This book, like its predecessor, is set in an Alternate Universe.

The characters in it aren't on our Earth. It's possible that they exist in a parallel dimension on many other planets called Earth, but they're not people with the same name who live on our Earth. Let me make that quite clear.
What happens in this book doesn't happen in our universe.

The way people behave in this book is no reflection on the behaviour of any similarly-named person here, on this earth.

It's just a story ... and probably not a very good one but, hey-ho, I DONE ME BEST!!

Oh, and this book may be too complex for a 6-year-old, possibly have too many BIG words for a 11-year-old, and is definitely TOTALLY UNSUITABLE for grown-ups!!!

Finally, BE WARNED - whatever you read in here DON'T TRY IT AT HOME!!

1

When a boy is 6 years old, I'm guessing that the most important person in the world, to him, is Dad.

Maybe Mum, because six is not that old (although it sometimes feels it when one is SIX!) and Mum is the person who has fed, clothed, loved him from the very day he was born ... and for all those long months beforehand.

When a boy is 11 years old, I'm guessing that the most important person in the world, to him, is Dad.

Mum. of course, comes a very close second indeed (often first!). Dad wins by a whisker because, when a boy has achieved double figures, it's Dad who is his action hero. Mountain biking, playing footy and all of those adventurous, exhilarating outdoor exploits at which Dad excels.

So, if we begin at the beginning, with Dad as THE HERO to two boys it may help you, dear reader, to understand this story. And there is something to understand.

Because Rex and Ran realised, one horrible day, that there was something dreadfully, dreadfully wrong with their Dad.

It was an overcast day. It was pretty miserable. Rain was in the air. It was cold. It was muddy. It was exactly the sort of day when reasonable people, given the chance, would stay indoors. A coal fire would be burning in the hearth. All the doors would be closed to keep out the cold or, better still, to keep in the warmth.

Rex & Ran Save Their Dad

There would be stuffed snakes along the bottoms of doors as draught excluders.

Old people, like Smelly Grandad and Fragrant Nanny would have extra pullovers on and a blanket over their knees. The radio would be playing and their dog, Meg, would be snoring quietly as close to the fire as she could get.

But, for Dad, Rex and Ran it was a day to enjoy being out in the rec[1] with a football, two pullovers as goalposts, and lots of steam rising from overheated bodies.

The joy of running and playing. The sheer pleasure of having Dad to themselves.

Except ...

Except, on that particular day, Dad called 'time' very early. Very early indeed. Why, the boys had barely started to glow, let alone sweat. Surely they had only been out enjoying themselves for seconds?

"C'mon, lads. It's time to take a break." Dad said.

Was that a wheeze in his voice?

A gasp as though he was out of breath?

A pant?

A rasp?

A croak?

Why was Daddy's face so red and his lips so blue?

"Do we have to, Dad?" said Rex.

"Yep. It's a bit too cold to stay out for too long." Dad said.

WHAT?!

---

1   Recreation ground

(Really)

Is this the man who jumped in a river in DECEMBER just because he could. Who climbed onto Fragrant Nanny's roof in JANUARY when it was snowing and he was wearing nothing more than a t-shirt, just to check a loose tile. A t-shirt on his top half. He did have trousers,socks and shoes on!

"Crikey blimey! I was just about to score." Ran complained.

Maybe he was, too.

We'll never know.

To say that the two boys were astounded would be an understatement. Always - I mean ALWAYS - it had been Dad who wanted to carry on.

Sometimes Mum had been forced to march down to the rec in her slippers and order Dad in. Usually because their lunch was spoiling.

On one memorable occasion, it had been Fragrant Nanny who had gone. Mum always needed to shout at them (well, at Daddy) but FN simply arrived, looked at them, and they'd immediately picked up their footballs and sweaters and gone home STRAIGHT AWAY.

Anyway, Rex and Ran are good boys so they trudged home with their Dad without too much grumbling and moaning and neither of them said either 'Crikey Blimey' or Blimey Crikey' even once.

But why had Dad wanted to stop playing?

And what on earth was wrong with his voice?

2

Smelly Grandad often went for 'a little lie down' in the afternoons because that's what very, very old people did. Although, to be fair, if the boys popped round he wouldn't bother, he'd play with the boys instead.

There wasn't too much physical exercise involved in that play but there was a lot a teeth grinding, almost always from SG. The grinding and facial grimaces[2] tended to take place when he'd lost at chess AGAIN.

Not only lost AGAIN but lost AGAIN after falling for THE VERY SAME MOVES. Bang goes the QUEEN.

If you, reader, thought that the scowls, frowns and pouts were any lighter when Ran won, you're sadly mistaken. They were worse.

LOSING TO A SIX YEAR OLD.

Anyway, at this point we're not interested in SG losing YET ONCE MORE at chess.

We're concerned with the fact that, just like very, very old people, including Smelly Grandad, Dad went for a little lie down as soon as they got back from the rec that day.

Was he ill?

Judging by the anal eructations[3] that roared out of his bedroom,

---

2   signs of a poor loser. Lighten up, Smelly Grandad!

3   farts

(Really)

he might, just possibly have been very ill indeed.

Ran didn't even need to press his ear to the door to hear them clearly.

And, was that Daddy moaning in between his flatulent[4] toots? It jolly well sounded like it!

Was it possible to trump whilst fast asleep? Ran thought he might try for himself.

'But' he wondered 'how would he ever know?'

Rex and Ran sat in their kitchen, with their cowboys and indians[5] on the table to play with and a nice, refreshing glass of water each to tide them over until lunchtime.

Their kitchen was the warmest, snuggest room in the house. It was a favourite room - after their bedrooms, living room, Fragrant Nanny's entire house and Smelly Grandad's shed.

"What's wrong with Daddy?" Ran asked in a whisper.

"Nothing!" Rex scolded. How could there be anything wrong with Dad? He was ... well ... DAD.

"Why was he grunting and making funny noises, then?"

"I don't know!"

"Why did his face look like a lump of beetroot?"

"I don't know!"

Ran took that to mean that Dad was SICK. Rex was 11 after all and if he didn't know why Dad had been making those worrying, scratchy, hoarse, nasal sounds and why his face was

---

4   farts

5   toy figures popular in the 1950s and 1960s.

the same colour as a tomato then things must be PRETTY SERIOUS. It certainly sounded serious. It looked to Ran as though Dad had just run about a thousand miles which, Ran knew, Dad could do any time he liked.

"Perhaps Mum knows." Ran said.

"Well, if she does and it's grown-up stuff she won't tell us, will she? She'll just pretend there's nothing wrong."

"Shall we ask her anyway?"

"Mum?" Rex yelled.

"Yes, my little pumpkin?"

Rex wondered if his Mum would EVER realise that he was ELEVEN YEARS OLD and his little pumpkin days were gone forever.

"What's wrong with Dad?" he asked.

"Nothing, pumpkin."

"Why did we have to come back early?"

Mum didn't answer.

"Why has he gone to bed?" Ran asked.

"I expect he's just tired," Mum assured them "he does work very hard."

"Told you." Rex whispered.

(Really)

3

To know - or think you know - that your dear Dad is poorly is a terrible, worrying state of affairs.

The boys talked it over that night in their bedroom.

Rex did most of the talking.

Actually, he did ALL of the talking because, after only a couple of minutes Ran was warmly ensconced in The Land Of Nod.

Rex soon realised that he wasn't going to get any answers from his younger brother because that individual was FAST ASLEEP.

Unusually, Ran was not only first asleep but first awake as well. Normally, it was Rex who was up and about first - often before Mum and Dad.

This time it was Ran.

And he BOUNDED out of bed and raced into his parents' bedroom, determined to jump straight on top of Daddy and give him a good (though nice) scare!

And he succeeded!! Daddy woke up instantly and immediately used a word that Ran had never heard before. It sounded like a really important word and Ran hoped that he'd remember it so that he could use it himself at a later date.

Unfortunately, he was sidetracked straight away so that

particular word[6] was forgotten.

What diverted his attention was (dear reader, I can hardly bear to tell you ... those gentlemen of a nervous disposition, ladies, children and servants should skip to Chapter 4 immediately!) a sight that small children should never have to see.

For Daddy's blue and white striped pajamas were slightly askew and sticking out for all to see was something so horrid that Ran stopped his bouncing and just ... STARED.

It was something soft, floppy and awful!!!

Something that could give little boys nightmares.

Something that struck a normally chatty little boy absolutely dumb.

Something unbelievable.

Something horrendous.

Something unreal.

Something that was ... ugh ... I'm shuddering just writing about it.

Take a breath!!

Ran couldn't take his eyes of the wobbly, meaty paunch that was quivering right in front of his eyes.

It was ... it was ... dare I say it? A big, fat belly.

NOOOOO!!!

Daddy, Mr Perfect, suddenly, almost overnight, had sprouted a great, huge, floppy belly.

Where had all the muscles gone?

---

6   he did use it when he was 24 years old and his girlfriend slapped his face. Ummm! Perhaps it was just as well he'd forgotten it for so many years!

(Really)

Ran's flabber was gasted. Shock, amazement, dumbfoundedness all struck him like a hammer blow. It was too much for a 6-year-old and Ran, much to his surprise (and Daddy's!), burst into tears.

"Oh, Ranny! Whatever's the matter?" asked Dad.

Ranny couldn't speak.

"It doesn't matter, Ranny. You didn't hurt Daddy ... not much anyway."

Ranny couldn't speak. He was far too busy doing hiccoughy sobs. His whole body was quivering. Tears gushed out of his eyes and rushed down his cheeks like a waterfall.

He was upset.

Daddy was FAT!

There was no other word for it.

FAT!

Of course, he couldn't say anything to his Daddy about it, so he mooched off to his bedroom and sat on Rex's bed together with his sobs and his heartbreak.

Once, not so long ago, he'd seen a little boy just about his own size and had tugged his Mummy's hand and asked (in a rather loud voice) "Mummy, why is that little boy so FAT?"

Of course, it isn't polite to say things like that. Each of us is different and, if some are larger-bodied than others, well, it's all part of the wonderful variety of humankind.

Which Ran's Mummy explained to him.

It was like some people had brown eyes, some blue and some a sort of greenish colour. No two people were the same.

Rex & Ran Save Their Dad

A bit like hair colour - sometimes fair, sometimes dark, or ginger, or straight, or curly, or, occasionally none at all.

"Like Grandad?" Ran asked.

"Just like Grandad." Mummy agreed. She was pleased that her little boy understood how varied people were and that it didn't matter one little bit.

"And smelly, like Grandad? I bet some people are." Ran said.

"Well," said Mummy, "if they're homeless, or don't have baths, or have some sort of disease, or don't ever change their underwear, or sweat a lot, or are overweight, or have an infection, or eat a lot of cabbage, baked beans, garlic, curry, and spices. Oh, and if they drink a lot of alcohol. Or grow a beard and don't wash it."

"Gosh!" said Ran "Grandad's not homeless, but I bet he's got all the rest of that lot."

Ran's Mum immediately set the record straight!!!

"Don't be silly, Ran!" She scolded him. "Grandad doesn't drink alcohol."

"I'm going to ask him if he ever changes his underpants." Ran said.

Well, that chat with Mummy had certainly helped Ran understand what RUDENESS was.

It would be VERY RUDE INDEED to ask Smelly Grandad if he ever changed his underpants.

It would be VERY RUDE INDEED to ask him if he had some sort of disease or if he ate a lot of cabbage and baked beans.

(Really)

And, it was BAD MANNERS to comment on another person's body shape.

Ran couldn't tell his Dad - his OWN Dad - that he thought he was FAT.

But he could talk to his older brother and see if, between them, they could SORT SOMETHING OUT to make him UNFAT. After all, they'd practically, nearly almost, saved the world from overheating and forcing everyone to live on hills or under water.

Practically.

Nearly almost.

Saving Dad would be a doddle[7] by comparison. Easy-peasy lemon-squeezy!

The boys could do it!

---

7   Doddle - a piece of cake ... hopefully lemon drizzle, my favourite!

4

A first hurdle ...

Rex, aged 11, and therefore quite intelligent and worldly-wise didn't believe his little brother.

Daddy FAT?!

Not in a million years!

Not in a million, zillion, squintillion, gazillion years - and that's an awful long time. That's longer than Nanny and Grandad have been alive even if their ages are ADDED TOGETHER.

"I saw it!" Ran insisted.

He and his brother were playing on their trampoline.

Unsynchronised bouncing[8] up and down made talking difficult, but it was a jolly good way of chatting about SECRET things without Mum and Dad suspecting a thing.

"No, you didn't!" Rex insisted.

"I did!"

"You didn't!"

"I did!"

"You didn't!"

"I did!"

"You didn't!"

"I did!"

"You didn't!"

---

8   When one was up he was up and when one was down he was down, and sometimes neither one was up or down.

(Really)

See - VERY secret things!

And Mum and Dad completely oblivious to every word!

Rex realised that each of them was speaking when they were highest in the air.

Spooky!

And very time-consuming. Five minutes to get four words out.

And exhausting. Two thousand calories to get four words out.

At that rate, they'd fall into a debilitating coma[9] before they'd reached any sort of agreement.

"I did!" yelled Ran.

And his big brother kindly let him have the last word.

Rex realised that, being almost twice as old as his brother - or, to put it another way - his brother being roughly half his age, that he was clever enough to get the evidence for himself. If there was any evidence, that is.

The beauty of having an 'open door' policy in Rex and Ran's house was that ANYONE could wander in ANYWHERE at ANY TIME.

This was not a state of affairs with which Nanny and Grandad were enamoured[10].

It was, however, very useful for Rex who simply popped in to the bathroom whilst daddy was taking a shower.

He only needed to be in there for a few seconds in order to find

---

9   worn out and fast asleep!

10   Nanny and Grandad had a 'closed door' policy as well as a 'clip around the ear' policy.

out the dreadful truth.

When he sat down with his little brother, at the bottom of the garden, behind the shed, he was actually shivering.

Ran held his hand.

"What did you see, Rexie?"

"It was horrid!"

"What?"

"You were right, Ran. Dad is FAT!"

Both boys sat silently for a moment, clutching each others hands, as they pondered on the enormity of it all. The enormity of, probably, the worst moment in their lives.

"That's not all." Rex admitted.

"What?"

"There was a Boa Constrictor in the toilet. Down the bowl."

"A bone an' a stricter? Yuk!"

"It might have been an Anaconda." Rex admitted.

"An an anna wotsit? Yuk!"

"You know what that means, Ran?"

"Check down the loo very, very carefully before you sit down?"

"No. Remember the rule - 'If it's yellow, let it mellow. If it's brown, flush it down' - well, the thing, probably a Reticulated Python, was brown. Why hadn't Dad flushed it down?" Rex spread his hands wide in a generic 'I don't know what's going on' gesture.

"What is an an anna wotsit? Or a red tickle hated wotsit?"

"Snakes!" said Rex.

(Really)

"Yuk!"

"It makes you wonder, doesn't it?" said Rex.

"Wonder what?"

"Why."

To say that Ran was totally flummoxed and confused would be a gross understatement.

What had snakes down the loo got to do with Daddy being FAT?

"Anyway," said Rex "it may not have been a giant snake at all. Maybe it was just some poo."

"No," Ran disagreed "it was much more likely to have been a snake. A giant red tickled one ... probably!"

"Huh!" Rex huffed dismissively, "You didn't even see it."

"I don't believe you anyway about snakes in the loo. You didn't believe me when I said Dad was FAT."

Moments before Ran said that, it did look as though a heated argument might have been about to kick off.

Now, though, both lads had their minds firmly back where they should have been all along, namely, on their FAT DAD.

What did a FAT DAD mean?

5

Imagine, if you can, if your imagination can possibly stretch far enough, if your wildest dreams could stretch and stretch until they become a THOUSAND TIMES wilder, what it would mean to two healthy little boys to have a Dad who SUDDENLY became FAT!

I know, I know, it's actually unimaginable.

Impossible.

Never happening.

Not in a million years.

And - as we've already said - not in a million, zillion, squintillion, gazillion years - and that's an awful long time.

However, let's try really hard and if we're indefatigable it may be practically manageable to imagine the unimaginable.

All those wonderful, special activities boys do with their FIT Dads.

NOT ANY MORE!

So ...

No more mountain biking.

No more football.

No more swimming.

No more rugger,

No hiking,

No playing 'King Of The Bed',

No rough and tumble,

(Really)

No playing catch,

No camping,

No trips abroad,

No being carried on shoulders.

A dreadfully depressing, awful list that included absolutely EVERYTHING two boys loved to do.

Rex and Ran thought they might just as well shove their heads down the loo and let themselves be gobbled up by the red tickle hated snake!

NO THEY DID NOT!

THEY THOUGHT NO SUCH THING!

THEY HAD BRAINS, IMAGINATION AND DETERMINATION!

They were going to save their Dad by UNFATTING him!

6

Their first task was to discover why Dad had suddenly become flabby, portly, corpulent, fleshy, pudgy, blubbery and FAT.

Who better to help them than Wise Grandad.

Even if that meant the torture of having to sit on the most uncomfortable chairs in the whole world for hours and hours and hours.

Mum kindly agreed to escort them to Wise Grandad's home. It gave her an opportunity to take him a selection of home-made goodies as he lived alone and she worried - like any loving daughter would - that he was not getting enough to eat.

The boys, doubling as pack animals for the trip, carried most of the goodies, and wondered if it was all worth it. Surely it would be less effort to just let their Dad get FATTER and FATTER and FATTER and FATTER.

Mum had packed: Vegan Enchiladas with Pumpkin and Black Beans; Lasagna (no need to keep repeating the word 'vegan' as it's all vegan [whoops! Just repeated the word ... never mind!]); Quinoa Casserole; Autumn Squash Wild Rice Bake; Jambalaya. That last one was a 'speciality' and just oozed with flavour and goodness - onion, garlic, celery, peppers, mushrooms, tomatoes, oregano, basil, paprika, Cayenne pepper, kidney beans, soy sauce and rice. Yummy!!

Far, far better for health and well-being than Dad's 'normal' meal of fried food - pork sausages, streaky bacon, baked beans, tomatoes, fried bread, fried egg, black pudding, white pudding, mushrooms, kidneys, hash brown, bubble & squeak, melted cheese on top, and, of course, tomato ketchup and brown sauce standing by, right next to salt, pepper and vinegar.

Double Yummy!!!

Hang about a bit!

Hold up!

Just a mo!

Sit tight!

Hold your horses!

Wait a sec!

Wise Grandad is NOT FAT. Dad is VERY FAT[11].

Wise Grandad eats small portions of vegan food. Dad eats massive, gargantuan, unbelievable helpings of fried food.

'I wonder ...' thought Rex.

Even though he was wilting beneath his burden of food, his active brain was still working hard.

'I wonder ...' thought Ran.

Even though he was wilting beneath his burden of food, his active brain was still working hard.

Rex's wondering was concerned with the apparent fact that his Dad might, just might, be eating too much and that could, perhaps maybe, be why he was getting FAT.

Ran's wondering was concerned with the apparent fact that he might drop down from exhaustion before they reached Wise Grandad's home!

11   Well, getting rather stout. Not quite very fat. YET!

Rex & Ran Save Their Dad

Why did he always get the heavy stuff to carry?

Didn't Mum even remember Smelly Grandad's maxim 'always wear the old ones out first'?

Thankfully, they arrived at their Grandad's home before Ran collapsed from sheer exhaustion and, for the first time ever, after Mum relieved him of his cargo, he was quite glad to plonk himself down onto one of those incredibly uncomfortable chairs.

Not for long! He was very soon squirming about wishing that they could go home.

"Grandad," said Rex.

"Yes." said Grandad.

"Why do some people get fat?"

"Well, there's a question." said Grandad.

Rex knew that, of course.

"Why do some people get fat?" said Grandad.

"That's what I just asked you." said Rex.

Grandad thought for a moment. "No," he said "I definitely remember saying that."

"Yes, but I'm the one who wants to know." insisted Rex.

"What a coincidence! We both want to know the same thing. Well I never." said an astounded Grandad.

"So why do some people get fat, Grandad?"

"Jamabalaya."

"What?"

"I'm not at all sure I've ever had Jamabalaya before." said Grandad, holding up the plastic freezer container neatly

(Really)

labelled by Mum.

"Grandad ..."

"Yes ... err ... Rex, isn't it?"

"I just wanted to know how it is that some people get fat and others don't."

"Goodness me." said Grandad. "I was wondering the same thing. What do you think the answer is?"

"I don't know, Grandad. I was sort of hoping that you might know." said Rex.

What a patient boy.

He's not even squirming in his seat like his brother.

Oh, hang on, he's sitting on the floor.

I suppose that's what comes of being almost twice as old as his brother - or, to put it another way - his brother being roughly half his age. So many extra years of knowledge and learning. And a bottom that's not quite as bony belonging to a boy who has LEARNED HIS LESSON the hard way after spending a lot more time sitting on those incredibly uncomfortable chairs. In fact, he's probably spent nearly twice as long as Ran sitting on them. Or, to put it another way, Ran has possibly spent half as long as Rex wriggling on them, completely unable to get remotely comfortable.

"Where were we?" asked Grandad. "I know we were having a lovely chat about something ..."

"Fat, Grandad."

"Hardly. I think you must be mistaken there." Grandad scoffed.

"No, not you. How do you stop someone getting fat? If someone is fat, how do you make them be skinny? If you don't want them to be fat, how do you help them get slimmer or slendererer?"

"Now, there's a question." said Grandad.

Ran piped up, "Can you answer it then, please, Grandad. Because my bum is getting really sore and achy."

"Actually," said Grandad, "I was wrong. It was three questions, wasn't it? So, why don't we take them in order?"

"Good idea." Rex agreed, hoping against hope that Wise Grandad would start being wise and just GET ON WITH IT!!!

"Only," said Grandad, "it does depend which question you actually want answering. Is this person already fat? In which case question the first doesn't apply, does it?"

Rex had forgotten what question the first was.

He was also rapidly losing the will to live.

"Grandad!" Ran said in a VERY loud voice, "This is the question. Someone is FAT. How do we get them NOT FAT?"

"Gracious," said Grandad, blinking, "there's no need to shout."

They were all silent.

Mum was quietly storing the meals she'd brought in her father's nearly-empty freezer.

Ran was silently wondering if his bottom had disappeared as he could no longer feel it. At the very least, he had a numb bum!

Rex was dumbly trying to decide if the worst torture was

(Really)

sitting on one of Grandad's chairs, or on the floor (more about the floor later!) or whether it was trying to get a proper answer to an easy question. Okay, the answer might not be as easy as the question, but he hoped that it would be HELPFUL.

And he really, really hoped that it would come pretty jolly quickly so that they could GO HOME.

"It's all about willpower." said Grandad ... at last.

"Gosh!" said Rex. "I'll never be fat then because I've got oodles of willpower."

Did Rex actually say that, or did he just think it? Was he actually considering the self-control and incredible willpower needed to stop himself shouting 'FOR GOODNESS SAKE, GRANDPA! ANSWER THE BLINKING QUESTION!'

No, he didn't just think it.

He did actually say it for real.

Out loud. Well, very quietly out loud so Wise Grandad may not have heard it.

It was Ran who thought it and DIDN'T say it out loud. He just thought what an incredible feat of patience and willpower it was to sit on that awful, dreadful chair without SCREAMING.

"You must," added Grandad, heedless of the thoughts of his two grandchildren, "have the determination and strength of will to eat less and to stop eating before you are full."

"What if your plate's not empty." Asked Rex.

"Start with less on your plate. That's what I do." Grandad told him. "Sometimes, I exist for an entire day on two peas and a glass of tap water."

"Grandad!" warned Mum.

"Err ... not that you boys should EVER try that!" He said, wagging his finger at them.

"I sometimes only have two pees in a day." Rex boasted.

"Grandad's NOT talking about those sort of pees. He's talking about the green peas picked from the garden." Mum told him.

"What," said Ran, "like minding your 'Ps' and 'Qs'[12]? Those sorts of Ps?"

Mum just looked at him. Well, not a 'look', more of a glare.

Or a scowl.

Or a glower.

Ran decided to shut up and not worry about any sort of peas but, instead, worry about how on earth he'd live without a bottom. His had gone for sure. Disappeared. Dare he try to stand up or, without a bottom, would his legs fall off?

When those two boys walked home from Wise Grandad's with their Mum they were disconsolate. Which means they were upset and completely fed up.

Well, not COMPLETELY fed up. Ran was pretty jolly happy because his bottom HAD COME BACK. And his legs hadn't fallen off.

Rex was pretty jolly happy because HIS bottom hadn't stuck to Grandad's old carpet.

The carpet that had tacky, glutinous STUFF embedded in it.

---

12   That means be on your best behaviour - especially around Grandparents!

(Really)

The carpet that was over 70 years old and, like Rex and Ran's two Grandads, past its best and full of all sorts of agglutinative[13] rubbish.

The carpet that was just vaguely, slightly, marginally better than sitting on one of Wise Grandad's excruciatingly uncomfortable torture chairs.

The boys' fedupedness was because they'd not got one step closer to solving the problem of their Dad's FATNESS.

So, the obvious answer (and one they perhaps should have thought of first) was to pop across the road from their house and interrogate Fragrant Nanny and Smelly Grandad.

And that is just exactly what they did.

---

13   Just a posh word for STICKY.

7

Fragrant Nanny had Welsh cakes, chocolate biscuits, delicious non-fizzy drinks and very, very, very comfortable chairs.

She and Grandad didn't mind how the boys sat, or sprawled, as long as they didn't mind sometimes sharing with Meg, the dog.

Rex and Ran didn't mind at all - as long as they didn't have to share ALL of their biscuits with the dog as well.

And as long as they didn't mind a bit of dog-dribble on their clothes. Which they didn't.

Grandad, looking very displeased, was busy setting up the chessboard whilst the boys lounged on the sofa.

Let's be absolutely certain about something here.

Both boys loved ALL of their grandparents.

What is true, however, is that, like all boys, I suppose, they preferred to be comfy and well-fed than being discombobulated[14] and starved.

A life of plenty and indolence is always the easiest and, sometimes, the most rewarding. Sometimes.

"Grandad?" Asked Rex, with crumbs of Welsh cake ejecting themselves from his mouth. Lucky Meg. A single crumb is very welcome to a starving animal.

"What now?!"

"If I ask you a question, will you give me a QUICK answer?"

"Go on, then." Grandad said.

---

14   Uncomfortable.

(Really)

"If someone's already fat, how do they get slimmer?"

"Thaaat iisss aaa goood quessssstiooonn." said Grandad.

He was just trying to be funny by giving a slow answer.

Sometimes Grandad's sense of humour was so very personal that not a single living soul understood it.

Quite how Fragrant Nanny had put up with him for MORE THAN HALF A CENTURY was a complete mystery to everyone ... including Grandad.

"And what's the answer?"

"Simple. Less food, more exercise. Oh, and lots of willpower."

"What if the fat person doesn't want to eat less food and take more exercise? What if they don't have any willpower at all?"

Although none of that was very kind to Dad, it all had THE RING OF TRUTH.

"Well, you can't force anyone NOT to eat and you can't force anyone to exercise more. Basically, I suppose you're up a gumtree without a paddle[15]." Grandad said.

"Huh?!" Said Ran.

Which is not terribly polite. It's almost as bad as saying 'What?' or 'Ay?'.

Rex was thoughtfully mute for a few moments. His silence was helped by the fact that he had one final mouthful of Welsh cake masticating away in his mouth.

His silence was not helped in any way, shape or form, by Meg slobbering all over his third-best polo shirt.

That single crumb might indeed be very welcome to a starving

15   Just for Rex - an example of a Mixed Metaphor.

animal but let's not kid ourselves that Meg is even remotely close to actual starvation.

She is the best loved dog in the world.

Probably.

Well fed.

Definitely.

"So," said Rex, his mouth now cake free, "what do we do?"

"Seriously?" Asked Grandad.

"Very seriously." said Rex.

Ran nodded in agreement.

"Well," said Grandad "when I say you can't FORCE anyone, I reckon that is true. But, one way could be to remove temptation. If there's no food there, it can't be eaten."

"Good thinking, Grandad."

"Or a change of diet might do the trick."

"What's a change of diet, Grandad?" Ran wanted to know.

"Well, if someone's eating rubbish - like those sweets and chocolate you two like so much - you replace it with good stuff. No sweets and choccy, more Brussels sprouts and cabbage. No fried food and more cucumber and tomatoes."

The boys nodded.

"Now, who wants me to thrash them at chess?"

Two hands shot up.

Three people forgot about FATNESS for a time and two people really enjoyed their games of chess.

One person did not.

The muted sound of teeth being gnashed followed the boys

(Really)

across the road to their own house.

Rex and Ran were forming a PLAN OF ACTION.

8

It was NOT REX AND RAN'S FAULT that Smelly Grandad's faithful dog lay on her side, panting, with her eyes closed and a frown upon her forehead.

Several piles of partly-digested food lay around her, and Fragrant Nanny, kneeling beside her, cradling the suffering animal's head in her hands, mirrored the animal's frown as she nursed that lovely dog, worried that she'd somehow been POISONED.

Grandad, meanwhile, studied the piles of vomit and he, too, carried a frown upon his forehead. Was it poison that had caused his dog's illness?

Thoughtfully, Grandad pulled at his beard. He wandered around the regurgitated heaps and a low, barely-heard 'Mmmm' sounded in his throat.

"Someone's been feeding her sausages and bacon," he said. "and I'm pretty certain that there are bits of black pudding in there as well. And some meat that I can't identify."

Nanny stroked Meg's brow and looked up at Grandad. "Who on earth would feed her so much stuff. Poor Meggy!"

"Poor Meggy indeed." said Grandad "When I get my hands on whoever did this, it'll be Poor Them!" he warned.

At this point, dear reader, do not fear because it was NOT REX AND RAN'S FAULT.

(Really)

Not really.

Well, in the interests of honesty, it was Rex and Ran's fault.

But, as they did it for the best of reasons, was it REALLY their fault?

As they didn't realise Meg Dog would actually eat THE WHOLE AND ENTIRE LOT of the food they dumped in her garden was it really their fault?

Because it was STOLEN FOOD was THAT their fault?

Because they might just have saved their Dad's life was it their fault?

Yep! It was.

Rex and Ran had known Meg long enough to realise that Labradors ate and ate and ate and ate and ate and ate ANY food they could get their jaws round until they were so stuffed full that they could do no more than lie down next to mounds of food that an overloaded stomach had sicked back up.

And that's exactly what Meg was doing, just lying down feeling very sorry for herself in a doggy sort of way.

It had all, probably, smelled so nice. How could she have resisted it? Mind you, to dogs many, many sorts of dead or decaying matter smell good enough to eat. Bodies of animals that had been dead for days were scrumptious, even with loads of manky, unidentifiable bits in them so it's easy to see why sausages were a favourite.

When you've slobbered and salivated over animals that have popped their clogs weeks beforehand, or nibbled on a month old fallen apple, or hoovered up rabbit poo, then ANY FOOD that's nearly almost FRESH is like a taste of doggie heaven.

And it was not (so Meg thought) as if Smelly Grandad and Fragrant Nanny didn't practically STARVE her.

Why, she was only fed TWICE A DAY!!!

Apart from the bits of cheese she got when Grandad was making his breakfast. And the yoghurt of course. Not forgetting the lunchtime carrot and a bit more cheese. Oh, and the early evening treat. Don't forget the bits of cheese in the evening. Nor the sheep poo at Scolton Manor. And, in season, blackberries. And, in the school holidays, all the bits of snacks kids strewed just about everywhere outdoors. And bits of wood.

You might be beginning to see why that poor dog was always hungry. Why, she was practically starved on a daily basis.

But what on earth does any of this have to do with Dad's FAT PROBLEM?

Well Ran and Rex had actually been listening to Smelly Grandad and had come up with a plan. A Masterplan!

They would replace Dad's BAD food with some GOOD food.

Easy.

Peasy.

Lemon Squeezy.

And their first effort was Easy-peasy-lemon-squeezy.

Dad had cooked his own breakfast. As usual. In his own saucepan. As usual. With his special ingredients. As usual.

Just a little reminder, in case anyone has forgotten the mound of rubbish on his plate and on the table.

(Really)

Here it is:

Pork sausages (4), streaky bacon(4 rashers), baked beans, tomatoes (6), fried bread (1 slice), fried egg (3), black pudding (2 pieces), white pudding (1 piece), mushrooms (6), kidneys (1 spoonful), hash brown (1 spoonful), bubble & squeak (1 tablespoonful), melted cheese on top, and, of course, tomato ketchup and brown sauce standing by, right next to salt, pepper and vinegar.

Oh, and if we're being particularly pedantic, there was one knife and one fork on the table.

The marvellously lucky happenstance was that Dad farted before he could start his meal.

His knife and fork were poised. About to lance down, impale a sausage, cut and then enjoy.

Ran and Rex were watching carefully.

They were almost tempted to forget the whole business and just watch, with awe, as that massive mound of heart attack material disappeared like magic into their Dad's gaping mouth.

That fortuitous fart, though, had awoken something in Dad's brain. It had triggered an alert. An alarm sounded (in his head). It was the thought, almost expectation, that there might be a follow through.

Dare he risk it?

Perhaps not!

Dad laid his knife and fork down very neatly, 'harrumphed' and left the table to go to the loo.

Just in case.

Rex & Ran Save Their Dad

You never knew.

Better to be safe than risk unclean underwear.

His sons sprang into action as soon as they heard Dad's tread up the stairs.

Rex went to grab some 'good' food whilst Ran picked up the laden trough ... sorry, 'plate'[16], and left with it.

Rex filled a fresh plate very quickly with beetroot, carrots, grapefruit, radishes, strawberries, spinach, tomatoes and shredded turnip.

Ran - for want of a better idea - nipped across to Nanny and Grandad's house and tipped the contents of the plate into their garden. The empty trencher was considerably lighter on the return journey.

Question: who was the angriest?

Was it Nanny and Grandad upon finding that their lovely Labrador, Meg, had been poisoned by some awful, dreadful MURDERER?

Was it Dad upon finding that the gargantuan meal he'd so been looking forward to had been replaced with a heap of RABBIT FOOD?

Answers on a postcard, please.

And, just in case YOU are the culprit and are going to get that anger heaped on YOUR head, you might want to post your answer from somewhere A LONG, LONG WAY AWAY!!!

Well, I'll tell you the answer ... although they were ALL a bit miffed (to say the least!) it was Mum! Mum was the angriest.

16   Pigs eat from troughs, men dine off plates. Perhaps it was a trough, then?

(Really)

9

Now I know what you're thinking!

Surely Nanny and Grandad should have been the ANGRIEST because their dog might have died in agony.

If not, then surely Dad should have been the ANGRIEST because his belly was empty and he was starving.

Who was hungriest - Dad or the dog?

Mum was the ANGRIEST because, being Mum and knowing just about everything, she KNEW who was responsible for the whole sorry mess. Two boys who she loved dearly, that's who were responsible.

Two boys who, regardless of how much she adored them, would have to pay for what they'd done. And they'd have to pay IN THE WORST POSSIBLE WAY.

But only after confessing to Dad and to Grandad and to Nanny. For Rex and Ran, the confessions could be far worse than the impending punishment.

They knew that they would see a certain look in Nanny's eye that said, clearer than words, 'you've let me down'.

Grandad might put his arms round them and give them a hug but, deep down in their hearts, they would know how disappointed he was.

As for Dad ... how could he ever love them again?

As for Meg ... that didn't even bear thinking about. She might never, ever let them stroke her again. She might never, ever play with them again, or let Ran snuggle up to her in her bed.

Imagine how those boys felt.

They'd only been doing their best to help their Dad and now what a total mess they were in!

And their day got worse when they started their round of apologies. Nanny and Grandad gave them such looks that both boys burst into tears. Grandad did give them both a hug which made them both feel a tiny bit better, but they knew how saddened he was.

As for Nanny! Well, let's just say that it was the FIRST TIME EVER that they'd not been given biscuits and a refreshing drink.

What Rex and Ran were dreading even more was their Dad's face as he tried very hard not to show how let down he felt.

"Sorry, Daddy." bawled Ran. Yes, he was crying again.

"Sorry, Dad." said Rex. Not quite crying (he was 11 after all!) but his eyes were very red and I do believe his lower lip was trembling.

By the time their confessions were over, being sent to their room with no supper was more of a blessing than a punishment. Both of them just wanted to snuggle down, feel sad, and wake up to a new day that just might be a little better than this one.

Sometimes, no matter how big boys are, at heart they're just little boys after all.

Sometimes, no matter how much one tries to help, things can go terribly wrong and, sometimes, other people just don't understand.

(Really)

With a little bit of luck and a following wind, everything could have turned out very different indeed.

And let's just STOP right now and explain a few things about FAT.

Rex and Ran really didn't mind whether their Mum and Dad - or anyone else for that matter - were fat, thin, or somewhere in the middle.

Mums and Dads are loved exactly because they are just who they say they are - Mum and Dad.

No child in the world has ever NOT loved their Mum and Dad because they were fat, thin, black, blue, green, short, tall, bony, bald, ginger, left-handed, curly-haired, old, young, lanky, muscular, scrawny, elephantine, ponderous, lissome, skeletal, mesomorphic, ripped, supple, cadaverous, endomorphic, ectomorphic, runty, elfin, stunted, gargantuan, gigantic, busty, shapely, neckless, pigeon-chested, wizened, anaemic, pale, pasty-faced, gravid, little, pimply, receding, obese, bow-legged, top-heavy, attractive, presentable, tattooed, undernourished, hairy, graceless, stingy, pigeon-toed or clumsy.

No, the boys wouldn't mind ANY of those. Indeed, they may not EVER have noticed ANY of those.

What was most important of all was a Dad who could PLAY WITH THEM.

And a Mum who could HUG THEM and COMFORT THEM and LISTEN TO THEM.

That's what families are all about.

Rex & Ran Save Their Dad

That's what love is all about.

At least, it is until kids reach their teenage years and then, at some stage, there'll be: "I HATE YOU!" yelled at Mum or Dad.

Who will feel the worst when such a horrible and appalling thing is said?

Mum or Dad, who have always given their child unconditional love?

Or the teenager, who wished they could take the words back?

Yep. The teenager.

But, get ready, Ran and Rex, because that's what spots and pimples and body hair do to a chap who's growing into a MAN. Makes them awkward, snotty and sullen.

The good news is that kids normally grow out of it by the time they're thirty five or so.

Anyway, you get the picture, I'm sure.

An attempt at a good deed that went horribly, horribly wrong.

Mum and Dad awfully upset.

Fragrant Nanny and Smelly Grandad appallingly annoyed.

Ran and Rex lamentably wretched.

Meg ... well, not really bothered to be honest.

All in all, not a very good day for anyone.

(Really)

10

As you might imagine, Dear Reader, two boys arose the next morning determined to give up their idea of getting Dad slimmer and fitter.

Oh, deary me, no!

Don't you believe it!

Those boys have more guts and determination than that.

A plan won't be abandoned just because of a blip and a hiccup.

It's a brand new day.

The sun is shining.

Mum's got kisses and hugs to give away.

Dad's got ... BLAST! and BOTHER! Dad's got his usual breakfast in front of him.

The kitchen table is groaning under its weight.

Dad's stomach is groaning at the thought of demolishing it.

The boys are groaning at the horrific sight.

They've certainly got their work cut out!

There it is:

Pork sausages (4), streaky bacon(4 rashers), baked beans, tomatoes (6), fried bread (1 slice), fried egg (3), black pudding (2 pieces), white pudding (1 piece), mushrooms (6), kidneys (1 spoonful), hash brown (1 spoonful), bubble & squeak (1 tablespoonful), melted cheese on top, and, of course, tomato ketchup and brown sauce standing by, right next to salt, pepper and vinegar.

Rex & Ran Save Their Dad

Oh, and if we're being particularly pedantic, there was one knife and one fork on the table.

And a small glass of tap water.

Rex and Ran couldn't bear to watch.

Unfortunately, neither could they bear NOT to watch.

It was a wondrous sight to behold, yet completely awful at the same time.

Three breakfasts on the table.

Tofu Scramble on Rye Bread.

One Egg Shakshuka.

Super Megalithic Colossal Mammoth Belly Buster Fry-up Mark Two (Expanded).

Yep, Dad was eating tofu ... NOT!

That was Ran. Rex had the shakshuka. Guess who had the other one!!

Just think, if Dad had an ordinary, healthful breakfast, instead of his usual gargantuan pile of processed meats, he'd have TWENTY MINUTES of additional free time every day.

He wouldn't have all the cooking to do himself. Nor the clearing up, washing up, drying and putting away.

"Is that nice, Dad?" Ran had to ask.

"Deelish!" Dad mumbled.

"Shouldn't talk with your mouth full, Dad." Rex warned.

Dad poured another river of ketchup onto his plate, followed by two dollops of brown sauce and an eructation[17].

"How many calories are on that plate, Dad?" Rex wanted to

17   Readers with a good memory will recall that's a posh word for a belch.

(Really)

know.

"About a thousand less than there were two minutes ago." Dad smiled.

Neither Rex nor Ran found that even vaguely funny.

Six eructations and two farts later Dad was finished.

He pushed himself up from the table and it seemed to Rex as though that was quite an effort. And was that his chair legs creaking, or the table, or was it Dad's knees?

Dad cleared up his mess.

To be fair, he was not afraid of hard work.

He kissed his boys with rather greasy lips. Gave Mum a hug (Rex noticed that she couldn't get her arms right round Dad any more!). And off to work he went.

Well, Rex and Ran looked at each other.

Not a word needed to be spoken because they both knew that they'd set themselves a challenge that was almost as monumental as their Dad's breakfast.

The task of SAVING THE WORLD paled into insignificance compared to this job.

Still, they were undaunted and, with Mum's agreement, popped over the road to Nanny's house to do some research in peace and quiet.

Grandad would be out with Meg and Nanny would be busy in her craft room making something useful.

Busy or not, she certainly had time to provide snacks and a drink for the boys. Things were, it seemed, back to normal after yesterday's disasters.

Two rather clever boys soon found books in Grandad's study that were really helpful.

"Gosh!" said Rex. "Did you know that if you're really, really fat your life expectancy can fall by as much as TWENTY YEARS."

"What does that mean?"

"It means that you can die TWENTY YEARS EARLIER than you should."

Ran's eyes filled with tears. "That means Daddy could die before he's THIRTY."

"Not really. He's forty two already."

"That's old!" Ran cried.

"Imagine how old Grandad is then."

"Yes, but he's ALWAYS been ANCIENT. That's way older than old." Ran scoffed.

"Here's another thing. There are no obese centenarians."

"What?"

"No obese centenarians."

"I don't even know if you're speaking English." Ran complained.

"I think it means you can't obey a sentry. Hang on, I'll check."

Ran just sat quietly, frowning. His command of Double Dutch was nowhere near as good as his English. It wasn't even up to his Italian.

"Oh, no. My mistake." said Rex. "It means there are no people a HUNDRED YEARS OLD who are fat."

(Really)

"A HUNDRED YEARS OLD." Ran echoed. "That's impossible!"

"Well, it's not impossible. In Japan most people are a hundred years old. Their children have to stay at home to look after them, so other people have to work twice as hard so that nobody starves. Sometimes their children are over a hundred years old as well, so it's the grandchildren who have to stay home.

Imagine if we lived in Japan, we'd have to spend all our time looking after both Nannies and Grandads AND Mum and Dad."

"I'm glad we don't live in Japan." Ran said.

"Well, it would solve one problem. We wouldn't have to worry about Dad not playing with us, would we?"

"Yes, but he's not a hundred, so we'd have to wait for ... well, for YEARS ... or quite a long time anyway before he's a hundred."

"Fifty eight years."

What a clever lad Rex was, working it out so quickly.

"That means I'd be ... how old would I be, Rexxie?"

"Sixty four!"

"Sixty four!"

"Yep. And I'd be nearly seventy."

Sometimes, children have thoughts that are so horrible or incomprehensible that they shouldn't be uttered. This was one of those occasions.

Sixty four!

Seventy!

45

Rex & Ran Save Their Dad

Never in a million years! Well, in fifty eight years - which is nowhere near a million years.

Of course, it isn't true that most people in Japan are over a hundred years old, but Rex was starting to believe it. Ran, being almost half Rex's age, believed it unconditionally. Because his brother said it was true.

Maybe, by the time the boys are sixty four and seventy, it WILL BE TRUE. Who knows?

People are living longer.

Except in America, where there are so many VERY FAT people who, as we know, won't live to a hundred, that everyone WILL NOT be living longer. They'll be living shorter! Shorter but fatter. Like Homer Simpson but not as yellow. Probably not as yellow.

And now, reader, you will almost certainly be ready to hear all about the GRAND LOSING WEIGHT PLAN.

The PLAYING WITH THE KIDS' AGAIN PLAN.

What have two boys (who once very nearly saved the entire world from disaster) come up with this time that will Save Their Dad?

Well, not just one plan, but a series of alternative plans, just in case the first one, by some strange and inexplicable reason, didn't work.

And, remember, before you read these ideas that Rex and Ran are two clever little boys. Don't discount any of their ideas just because YOU might think they're a bit silly. Some are a bit silly, but watch out for the ones that are a bit DANGEROUS!! There may well be some golden nuggets amongst the silly or dangerous ones.

Idea the first:

Liposuction. Scientifically sucking fat out of the body.

For - works quickly.

Against - Very, very expensive. Disgusting. Patient has to be in hospital. Sickening and stomach-churning (which is, I suppose a result of sucking out the fat).

Smoking. Sucking cancerous smoke into the body.

For - Doesn't involve invasive surgery.

Against - Very, very expensive. Disgusting. Person may not live long enough to enjoy their weight loss. Clothes stink. Inclined to cough up spit and phlegm. Fitness levels deteriorate, so no more playing with kids EVER.

Starvation. Not eating or drinking anything.

For - Very cheap with expenditure on meals down to NOTHING.

Against - Resultant weight loss will be only temporary as death will occur within three weeks.

Extreme exercise. Training all day every day.

For - Saves going out to work as there won't be enough time between training sessions.

Against - no time for playing.

Regurgitation. Sicking up food immediately after eating.

For - Historically important as Romans used to do it.

Against - someone's got to clear up the mess.

Laxatives. Eating 2 bags of liquorice after meals.

For - Liquorice tastes nice.

Against - Fairly painful when food passes out at the other end. Bummer!

Letting your stomach tell you when it's full.

For - Saves you having to think about not eating.

Against - Your stomach hasn't got a brain, so it's got absolutely no idea at all when you've had enough.

Clip your nose. Saves you smelling your food.

For - Your sense of taste is blunted, so you 'might' eat less.

Against - You'll look really stupid in a restaurant with a clothes peg on your nose. Your children will poke fun at you. You will never, ever be allowed to eat out in a restaurant with your wife.

Cleansing. Drink salt water each morning; a lime or lemon, maple syrup, cayenne pepper, and water concoction throughout the day; and laxative tea at night.

For - You won't need to worry about your mental state being stable, because it won't be.

Against - Everyone else will think you're mad AND you'll be pooing most of the night.

Divorce will follow, though whether that's a 'for' or an 'against' is for you to decide.

Prayer Diet. Constantly praying that you'll lose weight.

For - When you're praying, you're not eating (probably).

Against - your knees will be so bad that you'll NEVER play with your children again. You'll be hungry all the time.

Cabbage soup diet.

(Really)

For - Very low in calories. Cheap. Absolutely ANY other low calorie food will taste amazingly good. Anything at all that's NOT cabbage soup will taste amazingly good.

Against - You will never have a fart-free life. Everyone around you will stink. See earlier comment about divorce.

The Scotch Bonnet diet. Eat a Scotch Bonnet Pepper - or any of the following peppers before eating food:- Carolina Reaper, Trinidad Moruga Scorpion, Pot Dougla, Pot Primo, Trinidad Scorpion 'Butch T', Naga Viper, Ghost Pepper (Bhut Joloia), Pot Barrakpore or Pot Red (Giant).

For - It's cheap. All food will be totally tasteless, so you'll almost certainly eat less. You need never go to the dentists again as you will no longer be able to feel whether you've got teeth or not. You'll be able to light a wood fire simply by breathing on it.

Against - You will have to get used to living in agony, with your stomach crippled and your mouth, cheeks and nose completely numb and your eyes streaming 24/7. Your milk bill will soar to unmanageable levels[18]. The lining of your stomach may need to be replaced. Farting could cause death. Belching in company could cause death or impairment to anyone standing close to you.

What a load of old ... err ... great ideas!
And those are only the ones that Rex and Ran put on their shortlist.

---

18   Drinking milk is supposed to alleviate the burning sensation.

Rex & Ran Save Their Dad

Never mind the 'Fat Burning Underwear' or 'Tapeworm Tablets' or 'Jaw Wiring' or 'The Vinegar Diet' or 'The Belly Constrictor' or 'The Edible Bark Diet' or 'Clingfilm Wrap' or any of the many, many other silly ideas about weight loss that should have a DON'T TRY THIS AT HOME warning.

Most of those ideas are only tried by people with extremely small brains.

All are dangerous ... I mean both the silly ideas AND the people who might try them.

When I say 'What a load of old ... err ...' that's because, really, there are only two ways to lose weight. Here are four of them.

1. Eat less.
2. Exercise more.
3. Eat less and exercise more.
4. Exercise more and eat less.

Rex and Ran are pretty intelligent boys and how long do you think it took them to work out that there were many mad ideas, quite a lot of extremely stupid ideas and only a few GOOD ideas.

As ever, it's the most difficult ones that are most likely to work. In this life, hard work, application and a desire to succeed turn out FAR BETTER than hopeful and daft plans.

(Really)

11

One of the big advantages to Nanny and Grandad's house was that it was QUIET.

And peaceful.

And Nanny and Grandad would LEAVE YOU TO IT.

Plus the fact that Smelly Grandad, although he may not have been as sagacious[19] as Wise Grandad, would not only LISTEN to what small boys had to say but also suggest cogitations[20] that they could actually understand.

So, here's the question:

"Grandad. How do we get Dad to lose weight?" Rex asked.

Grandad had a bit of a ponder.

If he'd had a pipe, he might have smoked it.

If he'd had a visible chin[21], he might have stroked it.

If the log fire had been lit he might have poked it. Or stoked it.

Instead, he contemplated and ruminated instead.

Almost, but not quite, to the point where his grandsons worried that he might have forgotten their question.

Or fallen asleep.

"Well," he said at long, long last "I assume that your Dad doesn't particularly WANT to lose weight? That he's happy how he is?"

---

19 Same as 'wise' but posher.

20 Same as 'ideas' but posher.

21 He had a beard instead. Indeed, he may not have had a chin at all.

"Yes, Grandad." Two voices echoed.

"Well, it's obvious then, isn't it?"

"Is it?" Rex asked him.

"Well, your Dad doesn't want to change. Presumably your Mum doesn't want him to either?"

"We don't know, Grandad." Ran told him.

"Trust me. If your Mum wanted him to change, you'd have heard the nagging a mile away. It's a woman thing."

"What's 'nagging' Grandad?" Ran wanted to know.

"Crikey Blimey! Nagging! Cor! Bless my socks. There's a question."

Now Grandad sank into a reverie[22] and Rex and Ran waited … and waited.

"Nagging is an exclusively female pastime. There are Nagging Clubs all over the country, with competitions. Do you know what their slogan is? Well, I'll tell you. It's *A pugione numquam obliviscitur*[23] and that, boys, is Latin. You've heard the saying 'an elephant never forgets'."

They nodded.

"Elephants, believe you me, have nothing on Naggers."

And, strangely, Rex and Ran DID believe him.

"A Nagger goes on and on about something, usually to her husband. And when she's finished going on and on about it, she goes on and on again. And again. Until time immemorial. Forever."

---

22 Daydream.

23 'A Nagger Never Forgets.'

(Really)

"I don't think Mum can have been nagging Dad, then." Rex conceded.

"She has been nagging us about our bedroom, Rex." Ran said. "That's very true."

"So," said Grandad "if your Mum hasn't nagged him then there's only one surefire thing to try. Well ... pretty surefire. Well ... worth a try, at the very least."

Both boys, sitting cross-legged on the floor, surrounded by Welsh cake and biscuit crumbs, inched a little closer to their Grandad.

Meg, with her snout down to hoover up uneaten specks and particles, licked up near-invisible traces of food as though her life depended on it.

"Love." Said Grandad.

"Love?" Rex asked.

"Love?" Ran wondered.

"Love." Grandad agreed.

He sat back with a satisfied expression on his face.

The boys sat back with incomprehension on theirs.

"The Things We Do For Love." Grandad said. "As well as being a well-known song title[24], it is a true statement."

"I don't get it, Grandad." Rex said.

"All we have to do is show Dad how much we love him and remind him how much he loves us. It's worth a go. Not guaranteed but, if it doesn't work, I'm sure the three of us can come up with another idea."

---

24   By 10cc, a band from 1976, when Grandad was young. Younger anyway.

"How do we do it, though?" Rex asked.

"Very easy. As these things often are. K.I.S.S. - Keep It Simple, Stupid. Simple, easy plans are nearly always better than plans that are incredibly complicated and circuitous."

The boys waited patiently.

"Get your crayons out, and some drawing paper and you're going to make cards for your Dad. Not Birthdays cards. Not Christmas cards. Not Anniversary cards. Not Thank You cards. Your Dad needs to get a bit of a shock, so you're going to create some cards that are pretty darned horrible."

And that's just what his grandsons did.

When they left Nanny and Grandad's house to go home for tea, they left behind the cards they'd created.

Their part in the plan was finished and all they needed to do was to 'act the innocent' and pretend everything was completely normal.

As children, they had lots and lots of experience with acting as though they were innocent of EVERYTHING and were quite ready to plaster onto their cherubic faces an expression that said 'Who, Me?'

Gosh, they'd had enough practise!

Grandad realised he'd have to keep an eye on the boys. They were good lads but they were still children and might need a bit of a light shove in the right direction occasionally.

Some simple ideas given to them in words of one syllable or less.

Grandad smiled to himself as he recalled when Rex had been

(Really)

FOUR and he'd overheard Nanny and Grandad talking and COMPLETELY MISUNDERSTOOD some of the big words. He'd won a goldfish at the fair ... well, Grandad had won it really but it WAS Rex's even though he kept it at Nanny and Grandad's house. It was called Millie - after a floppy-eared rabbit in one of Rex's picture books.

Rex would spend hours, mesmerised, watching the golden fish swimming round and round and round and round in its little bowl. Gosh, he loved that tiny creature.

One day, Rex had thrown the goldfish out of Grandad's bedroom window.

Fortunately, it had landed in Nanny's little garden pond, right smack bang in the middle.

Unfortunately, it had landed in Nanny's little garden pond, right smack bang in the middle where the big rock was.

Nanny, being very kind, had fibbed a bit and told young Rex that his goldfish had swum down into the pond and ended up in a beautiful river where it lived happily ever after.

Grandad had been far more interested in why on earth Rex had chucked a harmless little fish out of an upstairs window.

And found out it was because of BIG WORDS that were MISUNDERSTOOD.

Rex had overheard his grandparents talking and misconstrued the meaning of a long word Grandad had said would really, really help his children and his grandchildren.

Hearing that ... well, sort of half hearing that - his number one Grandson decided to help make his Grandad's dream come true.

Hence 'Millie in the air'.

Well, if you can't work out for yourself what Grandad actually meant, then I've wasted several hundred words.

Grandad would keep an eye on the boys, help them as much as he possibly could and he'd start the plan with a chat with Dad.

(Really)

12

And Grandad DID set the plan in motion the very next day.

Now we're about to discover what was THE BIGGEST SHOCK of Dad's life.

When the hairs stood up on the back of his neck with FEAR.

Watch the trembling of his hands as he BEHELD the sight Grandad showed him.

See the TEARS in his eyes as the love of his children STRUCK HIM like a physical blow.

Note the DESPAIR in his heart as he realised how much he had let them down.

Imagine the AGONY that his own selfishness had caused.

Wonder at the PAIN in his heart.

Consider the PAIN in his belly ... but that one wasn't caused by Grandad's 'Big Reveal' that was due to OVER-EATING!! that very morning.

All (except for the last one) caused when Grandad popped round for a private chat with his son. He took with him several screwed up sheets of used drawing paper and a grim expression on his face.

Grandad hoped that the grim expression would help in letting Dad understand that Grandad wanted to discuss something PRETTY JOLLY SERIOUS INDEED.

The actual, true reason was because Grandad was about to tell his son a GREAT BIG, FAT, GIGANTIC FIB.

Rex & Ran Save Their Dad

To put it bluntly, he was about to tell a lie. And, as we should know, Grandad does NOT like telling fibs or lies or falsehoods or inventions or fabrications or untruths or canards or even sensational mendaciousness.

Well, if they were in a good cause, perhaps they might be excused.

In a VERY good cause, maybe fibs weren't so bad.

Although it is better not to tell fibs at all. Ever.

But Grandad was about to tell a MASSIVE one! And he was about to tell it in a very believable way. Well, he aimed to try his best to do just that.

"Hello, Dad." Said Dad.

"Hello, Son." Said Grandad.

"Sit yourself down and have a cup of coffee. Black? Six sugars?"

"Not for me, boy. I'm just too sad and upset to sit here drinking coffee." Grandad confessed.

"What's up, Dad? Anything I can do?"

Grandad didn't say anything. He just opened his fist and revealed the drawings he was carrying.

"Found these in the bin after the kids had gone." He said.

That is LIE NUMBER ONE!

Strictly speaking that wasn't a lie because Grandad had got the boys to put their completed cards in that very bin. Technically, it wasn't a lie ... except Grandad only 'found' them in the bin because he knew they were there.

"What are they?" Dad asked.

"Well, they're greetings cards. Sort of."

(Really)

Dad opened them out, flattened them and had a good look.

Unlike every drawing of his sons he'd ever seen, they were executed in just one colour.

None of the vibrant purples and yellows and mint greens and sky blues and carnation reds, not a one.

The sketches were in monochrome. If you don't know what that means, it means ONE COLOUR.

Worse still, that one colour was BLACK.

What sort of colour is that for a Greetings Card?

Oh, wait.

There's a picture of a gravestone.

There're letters on it.

R.I.P.

There are stick figures by the gravestone and drops falling from their eyes. Could they be tears? Could the drawings show sad people.

Oh, wait.

There are some letters as well. They're all over the cards.

Not terribly well executed. Not brilliant spelling. But the messages seems clear enough.

'Our Daddy'

'We miss you Dad'

'Always in our hearts' (Grandad had told them that one.)

"Hart fell colon own senses." An excellent effort by Ran and suggested by Grandad.

Dad looked at them.

Read them.

Just didn't understand them.

He frowned and looked at Grandad.

Grandad just shook his head from side to side.

"What are these?" Dad asked.

"Well, it's just a bit of childish silliness. You know how daft kids can be. The boys have got it into their head that you're going to die because you're getting so fat. I wouldn't worry about it, if I were you."

That is LIE NUMBER TWO!

Of course, saying 'don't worry about it' just made Dad worry about it.

He passed the cards from hand to hand, re-reading them over and over.

Grandad sat quietly, trying not to let his satisfaction show.

This idea might just work. Awful though it was.

One thing Grandad was absolutely, totally, sure of was that, if Nanny EVER found out it was HIS idea, he would be in SERIOUS trouble.

He'd be nagged like he'd never been nagged before.

He'd be nagged on a regular basis for the rest of his life.

For men of any age, there is not, and never will be, an antidote for nagging.

And ... men cannot nag back, it is just impossible, so Grandad couldn't get his own back.

He could see it now in his mind. Nag. Nag. Nag. Nag. Nag. NAG!

So, Mum's the word.

(Really)

And he really hoped that Ran and Rex would FORGET whose idea it was.

And he really hoped that the idea would help Dad jolly darned quickly.

"Where on earth did they get that idea from?" Dad asked, appalled.

"Haven't the foggiest." Grandad said.

That is LIE NUMBER THREE!

"I don't know what to say." Dad muttered.

"Nor me, son."

That is LIE NUMBER FOUR!

"I feel awful."

"Me too."

That is LIE NUMBER FIVE!

Is there no end to Grandad's fibs?

Will the boys ever believe ANYTHING Grandad says?

But ... most importantly at the moment, does Dad believe it?

Yes, he jolly well does!

An observer would be able to tell that straight away.

It's written all over Dad's face (well, not literally).

The horror.

The despair.

The very thought that his children - his very own, beloved children - think he's on a one way trip to HEAVEN. And all because he's getting a little bit chubby. Well, well-built really. Not fat. Not exactly. Nowhere near. Miles away from actually being fat. Just a bit more relaxed muscle than usual. Nothing a week, or possibly two, of exercise and the right diet won't put right.

There y'go, Dad. You really are thinking, in that little mind of yours, that you're not FAT.

Who are you kidding?

A week or two of exercise and dieting?

Unlikely. Impossible.

Dad, you're like an alcoholic who doesn't believe he has a drink problem, when EVERYONE else knows he has.

Dad, you're like a smoker who 'knows' he can give up any old time, but EVERYONE else knows he can't.

Dad, you're like a gambler who 'knows' he can stop any old time, but EVERYONE else knows he can't. Worse, the gambler knows for an absolute fact that he can win on the very next spin of the wheel, which justifies him putting more money he can't afford on number 13. Ohh! Lost again! Never mind, the next spin's bound to be a winner.

Dad, you're like a video gamer who 'knows' he can give up any old time, but EVERYONE else knows he can't. 'What? I've been playing for 14 hours without a break? Stuff and nonsense! Oh, I thought my watch had stopped.'

Dad, blah, blah, blah Shopping.

Blah, blah, blah Exercising.

Blah, blah, blah Social Media.

Blah, blah, blah Eating.

Hey! That's the one. Dad is addicted to eating!

But cannot change until he admits it.

(Really)

13

After a restless night, with not much sleep, Dad conceded defeat.

Yes, he finally admitted to himself, he was FAT.

Bleary eyed in the early morning, his tired brain had an initial problem to overcome.

"I'll just have a few cereals or something today, I reckon." He said.

Rex and Ran looked at each other over their dripping spoons and in that glance they saw the reflection of victory. Thankfully, they kept mum.[25]

Whilst Dad poured oat milk over his Weetabix, Mum looked at him. It was, in fact, one of her famous glares. Not quite as impressive as one of Fragrant Nanny's glares, but pretty intimidating nonetheless.

"What about your sausage and fry up?" She asked.

"Oh, I think I'll give them a miss. This is much healthier for me."

When Dad said that, he avoided looking at Rex and Ran. They avoided looking at their Dad, but they did look at one another. If looks could talk, they'd have been saying to one another 'Yay!'.

"Oh, you'll give them a miss, will you?" Mum asked.

---

25   They didn't keep their Mum, they didn't earn enough.

   It just means they remained silent.

Rex & Ran Save Their Dad

There was a bit of a warning in that sentence but Dad, bless him, didn't pick up on it. Silly!

"Yes. I don't need all that lot in my belly first thing. Anyway, a change is as good as a rest."

"You do realise that the freezer is stuffed full of food for me and the kids that I've bought whilst it's on offer, don't you?" Mum said, in a voice that could freeze barnacles on a rock. "You do realise that there's no room for your ... your ... FRY-UPS!"

"Sorry."

"Do you mean that you're sorry that you're wasting OVER A HUNDRED POUNDS WORTH OF FOOD?"

That was a bit of an exaggeration. A huge lump of an over elaboration. Dad's 'special' food was, though, darned expensive. Ran looked at his Dad. "You'd have been grateful for that in the war." He said with a smile on his cherubic little face. He knew that for a fact because Grandad had told him, countless times, that HIS Dad, Great Grandad Fred, used to say that.

"Shuttup, Ran! Eat your breakfast." Dad shouted.

Ran's smile disappeared to be instantaneously replaced with a look of complete shock and horror.

Rex kept his head down and his gaze firmly on his cereals.

Mum seethed with anger at the sheer wastefulness of food.

Dad simmered with rage ... and he was feeling a bit sorry for himself.

Gosh. It was only the opening seconds of the very first minute of the very first hour of the very first day of Dad's NEW

64

(Really)

DETERMINATION and everyone was miserable already.

Still, in a couple of weeks time, Dad would be slim and fit again, taking his kids out for play and exercise and everything would be back to normal.

Oh, to be such an optimist.

There speaks someone who has NEVER tried to lose weight.

Never been on a diet.

Never been obliged to eat food they absolutely HATE.

Never drank calorie-free green gunk that tastes of grass with rabbit poo embedded in it.

Never had their trousers fall down in public because they're too big. The trousers, that is.

Never smelled sausages and bacon frying without being able to devour them.

Oh, it's not easy UNFATTING yourself!!!

But, gosh, Dad had a lot of DETERMINATION and he really, really wanted to get some multi-coloured cards on his next birthday.

And he really, really wanted to get a next birthday.

14

Rex and Ran were very, very keen on helping their Dad.

Their first opportunity came sooner that they thought.

Dad was wearily chomping his way through his Weetabix and oat drink - no sugar - with a face full of distaste.

"How do you two fancy a day out bike riding with me?" He asked.

Really?

Did he need to ask?

Did he think they might not want to?

Not a chance!

"Yes, please, Dad!" Two voices cried in unison.

"I thought we might take the old van across to Wales and find a track."

"Yes, please, Dad!" Two voices cried in unison.

Dad smiled through a mouthful of cereals. Or it may have been a scowl. We can't tell.

Well, if he was pleased that his boys fancied the trip, then it was a smile.

If he was thinking about the taste of the oaty-flavoured Weetabix, then it was a scowl.

"Better get your bikes ready then. I'll nip across to Grandad's and see if he fancies coming with us and taking a few photos."

No sooner were those words out of Dad's mouth than Ran and Rex slurped up the last of their breakfast and made a headlong

(Really)

dash for their bikes. And their helmets and knee pads and elbow pads and safety glasses and padded gloves.

Some words were exchanged betwixt and between them when each commandeered items claimed by the other.

By and large, though, their excitement was more than enough to keep them friendly and to help one another prepare.

Mum, meanwhile, was packing them food and drink for their adventure.

Wow!

They had: .

Vegan gluten-free corn dogs,

Vegan pigs in a blanket,

Broccoli and cauliflower tots,

Chickpea, tomato and lettuce sandwiches on Warburton's[26] Seeded Batch Bread,

Vegan Brownies, and

Apple and Kiwi green smoothies.

Yummy!!

As well as towels, water and a change of clothes. Two changes of clothes in Ran's case. Just in case.

Considering the length of time it usually takes parents and children to get ready to go out, and how many essential items suddenly go missing and cannot be found, it is almost magical to know that the four 'boys' were being waved off by Mum and Nanny within the hour.

The old van gamely chuddered along. Dad and Grandad in

---

26   The author is not on a commission from Warburton's. Sadly.

the front and the boys playing 'I-spy' in the back, squashed amongst the bikes, food and backpacks, plus other assorted and indeterminate items relating to Dad's work.

It may have been a long and uncomfortable journey for Rex and Ran, but they' didn't mind because THEY WERE GOING ADVENTURURURING with their Dad.

And Grandad.

The Grandad whose bum was numb by the time they reached the border with Wales, and whose body had reached a state of light agony by the time they passed a signpost saying 'Merthyr Tydfil' 6 miles.

Rex and Ran, too, although neither boy was sure what a Merthyr Tydfil was, were cheered by Grandad's apparent pleasure at reading the signpost as they had long gone past cramp and boredom and were now visiting the doldrums of apathy[27].

Ran was white-faced as he did not travel well. Rex was fidgeting constantly to try and get even remotely comfortable for a second.

Not a great deal of imagination is needed to know that they were all DELIGHTED to reach their destination. The most marvellous bike-riding location in the ENTIRE COUNTRY.

"C'mon then, lads, let's get the bikes out and get ourselves sorted." said Dad.

"Where's the loo?" asked Grandad.

---

27   It doesn't matter how short or long a journey is, if kids don't fall asleep they get BORED and RESTLESS.

(Really)

"Where's the bike track?" asked Ran.

"Where's the food?" Rex wanted to know.

"Where's the loo?" Grandad asked again. It sounded urgent.

"Over there, Grandad." Dad pointed. "Or in the bushes, if you must."

"Is that the bike track?" Ran asked. He was first to get all his gear on (surprisingly) and itching to get started.

"I can't answer you all at once." Dad complained.

"Where's the food?" Rex asked yet again.

Dad WAS looking forward so much to being out with his boys, but he wished that Rex would, please, just shut up about food. At least, Dad thought, they hadn't got any PROPER food with them. So he wouldn't be tempted to overeat. Not tempted one little bit.

What a wonderful day they had!

Even their picnic tasted pretty good to Dad. Well, not bad. He even thought the dead fly on his chickpea, tomato and lettuce sandwich on Warburton's Seeded Batch Bread might have improved the taste[28].

The Welsh weather had granted them quite a lot of warm sunshine.

The bike tracks were 'brilliant', 'amazing' and 'stupendous' and it was generally agreed that a future visit would be a definite definite.

Rex and Ran, full of boundless energy, would happily have

---

28   That wondering ruins the author's chances of commission!!

stayed there for a week or more. The fun they had was immeasurable.

Grandad took more than three photos with his Kodak Brownie Six-20 D - cost £4 19s 11d - before his film ran out. He'd forgotten, in the rush, to bring any spare film with him. He had enjoyed himself and hoped that there'd be at least one photo where the subject's head wasn't chopped off. Full of positivity when asked, he secretly thought the chance of his one action shot being anything but a useless blur was NIL. His grandchildren cycled FAR TOO FAST.

Dad was exhausted.

He truly didn't remember cycling over rough ground ever being quite such hard work.

"Do you fancy driving back, Grandad?" He asked.

"Yes, I don't mind."

To say that Dad was immensely grateful would be an understatement.

After a quick visit to the loos, they were ready to leave. Then Grandad had to go back to the toilet for another go - just in case.

They heaved themselves, their bikes and their detritus wearily into the old van and tried to make themselves comfortable for the long trek home.

What a perfect day.

What a wonderful experience.

What a marvellous Dad.

What a kind Grandad.

(Really)

"Let's go home!!!" Grandad yelled as he switched on the engine.

Then he stalled the van (well, he wasn't used to it) to much hilarity from everyone. Except Grandad. He didn't see any cause for amusement.

Anyway, the good news is that their excellent day was not spoiled in any way, shape or form by Grandad's lousy driving and he only crashed the gears a couple of times before they were safely away from the bike track and back on the main road.

Did Dad complain even once about Grandad's driving? About the crashing of the gears?

No, he did not!

Grandad thought that was a bit odd. He would certainly have made some sarcastic comment if it had been HIS vehicle.

He looked over at Dad, about to mention it, but when he saw what he saw, he immediately forgot about his lack of driving skills.

Dad was slumped in his seat.

He was making small, guttural, groaning noises.

He seemed almost asleep ... or partly conscious.

His face was pale and sweaty.

Grandad carefully pulled the van over to the side of the road and stopped. His heart was in his mouth. He was trying to wrap his head around the fact that Dad might be under the weather. He felt like a fish out of water and knew he would

have to step up his game, go the extra mile and hang in there[29].
Dad's mouth was open and drool was slowly dripping out of it.
His breathing seemed difficult.
In short, he looked in a PRETTY BAD WAY.
What should Grandad do?

---

29   Lots of idioms especially for Rex.

(Really)

15

By a stroke of luck, the sort that often happens to authors of well-constructed stories, Grandad spotted a police car travelling towards him. Very quickly, he leapt out of the van and started waving his arms furiously.

He was desperate.

Oh, no! The police car sailed straight past him, leaving him standing there in shock. What next?

Oh, look, Grandad! The good old British police.

They were turning round and heading back.

Grandad quickly spoke over his shoulder to Rex and Ran.

"Just stopping for a quick wee, boys." He said.

Thankfully, Rex and Ran were both nearly asleep.

Grandad had never been happier to see those blue uniforms.

In point of fact Grandad had NEVER been happy at all to see those blue uniforms! Ever since the day he was stopped and asked if he'd been drink driving:

'When was the last time you had an alcoholic drink, sir?' asked the officer.

'1954.' Grandad told him, smiling.

'So,' said the policeman, looking at his watch. "Six minutes to eight. Hmmm ... and it's now just coming up to nine o'clock. Firstly, sir, it's no laughing matter, so you can stop grinning. Secondly, sir, the alcohol will still be in your system and you may well be guilty of DRINK DRIVING!'

'No, no! Not 19:54 o'clock! The year 1954.'

'Very funny, sir. Would you mind stepping out of your vehicle and blowing into this bag for me, please.'

By that time, Grandad didn't think it was a laughing matter[30] and, ever since, he's not really liked police officers that much.

The good news is that he's still got his sense of humour.

The less good news is that no-one understands it.

The even less good news is that Nanny, especially, doesn't understand a single one of Grandad's little jokes and bon mots.

Anyway, back to the serious stuff.

"Prynhawn da. Problem, sir?"

Grandad waved his hands to try to 'shush' the officer a little.

"My son's having some sort of funny turn in the front and I've got my two Grandsons in the back. Is there a hospital close by?"

The officer turned to his colleague in the car and made a telephone sign with his hand. "Ffoniwch Ysbyty'r Tywysog Siarl," he said. "Right, sir, you pop yourself back in your van and follow us."

With that, he trotted back to the patrol car, strapped himself in and then led Grandad's van away with their blue lights flashing in his eyes. Really annoying.

Thankfully, the boys remained in a lethargic doze and Dad didn't put Grandad off his driving by groaning too much. Although it seemed an awful long time, it wasn't many minutes before they pulled up at the emergency entrance to the Prince

---

30   He was as sober as a judge. That's a simile Rex!

(Really)

Charles Hospital.

Despite the seriousness of the occasion, it has to be said that Grandad quite enjoyed having a police escort and speeding past other cars and, at one stage, he found himself making little 'ee-aw' noises.

Thankfully, no-one else heard them.

He'd keep that bit to himself because some things, looking back on them, are just NOT FUNNY.

Several nursing staff and a stretcher were waiting for them as they drew up.

The kind police officer popped around to Grandad. "Here we are, sir. The nurses will look after your boy now."

"Thank you, officer. I can't tell you how grateful I am." Said Grandad. Well, he COULD tell him but, to be fair, poor old Grandad was in a bit of a state. Things like this just didn't happen to him on a daily basis.

His own son looking desperately ill and lolling about in his seat like an imbecile. Two little boys dozing in the back - about to be woken up to a scary scene.

Grandad would have to be tough!

Grandad would have to have a wee within the next few minutes!

"C'mon, sir. You get the boys and I'll take you in to see where your son's going. My colleague will park your van and come and find us."

"Thank you."

It definitely needs to be noted that those two kids were brilliant. At first, they didn't really know what was going on. Luckily, they didn't see their father strapped on to a stretcher and wheeled into the Emergency Department.

For small(ish) children who've just woken up fully in a strange place, they were remarkably well-behaved.

Being woken up next to ambulances and police cars MUST have given them both a great shock, but they remained calm and quiet.

Unlike Grandad, who was blathering like an idiot and pulling them quite forcefully out of the van.

Unlike Grandad, who was desperate to follow his son and the police officer - as well as pay a pretty urgent visit to the nearest toilet. But that would have to wait.

First things first.

Poor Dad. His stretcher raced along the corridor, through a crowded waiting room, and disappeared through double doors at the far side.

All of the waiting patients had turned to look at the stretcher and, now, everyone turned to gaze at the two little boys and the elderly man who wandered in accompanied by a uniformed police officer.

How Grandad managed to get to the counter and give all of Dad's details to the sympathetic lady there, I do not know.

He was in a perfect daze.

If only Nanny was here.

"Would you stay with the boys for a few minutes while I go to the loo?"

"Certainly, sir. I won't be leaving until I know you're ok and your van keys are back with you." The terribly kind officer told Grandad.

Two pale-faced, silent little boys sat very quietly with the policeman.

When Grandad returned, his heart went out to them. They looked so scared and lost and unhappy.

Grandad squared his shoulders, metaphorically smoothed away the frown on his forehead and straightened up as much as he could.

He tried to look positive and a lot more cheerful than he actually was.

"What's happening, Grandad?" Rex asked.

"The doctors are just doing a few tests on your Dad. He felt a bit poorly after all that cycling. It's probably to do with that picnic he ate - he's not used to that sort of food."

That was an attempt to inject a bit of humour into the occasion. Usually, Rex or Ran would be very kind and raise a bit of a smile when Grandad said something he thought was amusing. Not this time, though.

Two innocent little faces turned up to him and four slightly watery and very wide eyes looked at him for reassurance.

"Here y'go, sir. Your van keys."

"Oh, thank you."

"Now, when you leave, go straight across the car park to the very far side and that's where your van is."

"Thank you."

And that was about all Grandad could find to say. He just sat down on a hard chair and put his arms around two frightened little boys.

"Well, we'll be off, sir. Pob lwc! Hwyl fawr, blantos[31]."

And, with a reassuring pat on Grandad's arm and a smile for Rex and Ran, the two very, very kind police officers left.

Never, ever would Grandad EVER hear a bad word spoken about our wonderful constabulary in future.

Well, unless he got stopped again by the horrible, horrendous, abhorrent, blue-clad Gefreiters for something HE DIDN'T DO! Again!

The problems with looking after two children, by yourself, in a strange place, are multifarious.

Even worse if a body isn't used to looking after children-preferring instead that someone else - like Nanny, say - did the hard work and, if needed, a second person could be there as a sort of backup.

Children cannot be left alone amongst total strangers, some of whom in this Waiting Room looked untrustworthy. Not necessarily because they had blood on some part of their body, but because the smell of them was unpleasant. Therefore they might be equally unpleasant.

Some of them looked as though they didn't have the brainpower to be out by themselves. They certainly couldn't be safe with children.

Some of them looked as though they could well be under the

---

31 'Good luck! Goodbye, kids.' That's Welshish!

(Really)

influence of alcohol. That seemed particularly likely of the ones who were singing. It seemed absolutely certain of the woman sitting slumped on the floor next to a pile of vomit.

Grandad needed the loo roughly once every twenty minutes. That is one of the drawbacks of being elderly and having a small, weak bladder.

Each time, both Rex and Ran had to go with him. Thankfully, for a couple of those ablutions, the boys needed to go as well.

Not that they blamed their dear old Grandad.

No.

They were too busy worrying.

Neither of them dared to ask what had happened to their Dad.

They knew full well what hospitals were for and, specifically, what EMERGENCY hospitals did.

So they sat quietly, white-faced and worried.

Grandad sat with them, protecting them. He, too, was white-faced and worried.

Hours passed.

Ran and Rex got more and more fidgety. They couldn't help it. They're kids.

They had demolished several bars of chocolate EACH, drank half a dozen fizzy drinks and expelled about 40 litres of wee.

An hour seems an awfully long time when you're 6 years old and forced to just sit and wait. Although ambling about within Grandad's sight line was okay.

Three or four hours, even for an 11-year-old is a bum numbing amount of time.

But, weren't those kids and their old guardian as good as gold really.

Not one word of complaint issued from their lips.

Not one.

And, at long last, after they'd just about given up and resigned themselves to waiting FOR EVER, a man in green scrubs came out of the door that their Dad had passed through hours and hours and hours and hours before.

Oh, heavens!

Oh, crikey!

Oh, blimey!

Three worried chaps sat up straighter in their seats and glued their eyes on the medical man. He was heading straight for them.

Was that a slight grin on his face?

I don't think so!

It wasn't even a shadow of a grim grin.

He looked, Grandad thought, pretty darned severe.

"Hello." The serious looking doctor said, leaning down and addressing the boys. "I expect you want to know how your Dad's getting on? Well, he's fine. Absolutely fine."

Grandad felt his eyes getting damp. Were tears about to dribble out. Not to worry, Grandad was used to dribbling.

Rex and Ran were both very, very quiet and - yes! - those were definitely the beginnings of smiles on their innocent, eager little faces.

The doctor turned to Grandad. "We've just punched a few

(Really)

holes for him and he should be as right as rain very soon."

"Wha ...?" said a shocked Grandad.

The boys looked astounded and horrified.

"Yes. Quite simple really." The doctor smiled.

"Punched holes?!"

"Yes, that's all it needed. Amazing really."

"You punched holes ..." gasped Grandad.

The doctor laughed. "Well, not me personally."

"Who ... I mean you're a doctor, aren't you." Grandad asked.

"A surgeon actually." The doctor admitted. "But, no, I didn't do it. I got one of the porters to do it as he'd got a gimlet."

"Gimlet?" Poor Grandad could hardly speak.

"Yes. It's a woodworker's tool with a sharp, pointed end. Ideal for punching holes in things. I asked him to put two or three in, just to be on the safe side."

Have you ever seen a small group of white-faced people with their mouths hanging open and their eyes open so wide that it's a complete mystery why their eyeballs didn't pop out and roll away across the floor.

"Was my son under a local anaesthetic or a general one?"

The surgeon thought Grandad's question was extremely funny. If he'd been a jolly, rotund, Father Christmas type, fits of laughter might have found him joining the eyeballs rolling about on the floor.

He was, though, rather cadaverous, so a small 'hee-haw' sufficed. "Gracious me! No anaesthetic needed."

Grandad rose to his feet. He stretched himself up to his full height (which made him considerably taller than the surgeon!). He invaded the surgeon's personal space. He bunched his hands into fists. His tone, when he spoke through gritted teeth, was menacingly ferocious. "Do you mean to tell me that you've had someone with no medical training punching holes in my son AND WITHOUT ANAESTHETIC?!!"

The boys were still open-mouthed.

The poor surgeon began to smile rather broadly and I do believe he'd have roared with laughter if he hadn't caught the full impact of Grandad's face.

"Gracious me!" he stammered. "You've got the wrong end of the stick. My fault! My fault!" he hastened to say. "It wasn't your son our porter punched holes in ... oh, no. No! Indeed not!"

"What on earth are you talking about then?"

Grandad's fist was raised - as was his ire[32] - and he was just an inch from losing his temper and giving the man a periorbital haematoma[33].

"His belt."

"Ay? You what?"

The boys were still open-mouthed.

The surgeon pulled a chair up, so that the four of them could sit in a little square, cutting them off from others in the waiting room and affording them a semblance of privacy.

By sitting down himself, the man was using a bit of basic

---

32 Anger

33 Medical name for a black eye.

psychology. Grandad would almost certainly sit down himself and stop looming so threateningly.

Grandad knew a fair bit about psychology and was very, very tempted to remain standing. He didn't, though. He sat next to his two grandchildren.

The boys were still open-mouthed.

"I'm guessing that your son has put on a bit of weight lately?"

Rex looked up very quickly.

Ran shot up in his chair.

The boys were still open-mouthed. But they suddenly found themselves wide awake.

'Poo on a stick!' Ran thought.

'Galloping Gremlins!' Rex thought.

Grandad thought something entirely different. Luckily, we can only read the words written on this page and NOT the ones in Grandad's mind, so will NEVER KNOW exactly what he thought. If you, dear reader, had to take a random guess, it might well have been something that Nanny would have considered best to wash out of Grandad's mouth with a large bar of carbolic soap.

How on earth did the surgeon know that Dad was getting FAT?

Well, because he was a specially trained senior doctor. That's the first reason.

Secondly, he knew because Dad's trouser belt was SO TIGHT that the nurses very nearly had to cut it off!!

"Now," said the surgeon leaning closer so that he could speak in a low voice no-one else might hear. "as the gentleman's put on weight around his waist, his belt had started to act like a tourniquet around his gut. It disrupted the flow of his digestive system."

Grandad nodded and two boys looked flummoxed[34].

"It also has increased abdominal pressure, making it difficult for gas and food to move downwards."

Here, the surgeon turned to the two spellbound boys.

"I'll bet you haven't heard your dad trumping[35] quite as often as usual, have you?"

The boys didn't reply. Rex thought how wrong the man was. Lately, Dad had taken over from Grandad as the NUMBER ONE FART MACHINE. Although Grandad didn't seem to be giving up his title without a fart ... err ... without a fight.

Ran didn't really know what trumping was so he kept quiet. He did think it might have something to do with America, orange faces and bouffant hair, but wasn't sure what.

The surgeon took their silence as agreement.

"Well, what happens is that stomach acid can't go down, so it goes back up. That means the patient is much more likely to suffer heartburn and acid reflux. A tight belt also magnifies bowel discomfort and stomach aches."

Grandad nodded and two boys looked only slightly less flummoxed.

"The simple answer is to relieve the pressure. We've done that

---

34 Clueless.

35 Farting.

(Really)

by punching a couple of extra holes in Dad's belt. Now he's just having a gentle massage and he should then be perfectly fine to go home."

Now the surgeon did smile, hoisted himself to his feet and stuck out his hand for Grandad and the boys to shake it.

No doubt he had to rush off to an emergency and save someone's life, so wasn't it really nice of him to spare the time to talk to worried strangers.

Actually, his coffee was getting cold and he was jolly anxious to go and drink it.

Perhaps with a chocolate digestive.

If he was lucky.

"What's happening, Grandad?" Ran asked.

Grandad patted his hand. "Your Dad's going to be alright. We'll be on our way home very soon."

Rex, being almost twice as old as his brother - or, to put it another way - his brother being roughly half his age, he was clever enough to know that words like 'tourniquet', 'acid reflux' and 'abdominal pressure' were important and grave.

It didn't sound to him as though Dad was going to be alright. Not at all.

It sounded pretty desperate.

And it sounded jolly serious.

It sounded, in short, as though Ran and Rex were going to have to 'up their game' and come up with a significant plan to help their Dad.

16

"Just a bit of indigestion."

That's how Dad explained the Terrible Incident Of The Emergency Dash.

'Yeah. Sure.' Rex thought.

Ran didn't exactly know what indigestion was, but Dad didn't seem bothered so everything was okay.

Back to normal.

Good as gold.

Hunky Dory.

Balderdash and Malarkey.

Whoops! That last one was from Rex and as he sat, at the bottom of the garden, with his little brother.

"Not used to my new diet." Dad had said.

Malarkey and Balderdash. Phooey! Jumpin' Jehoshaphats! Good night! and Barnacles!

"It's nothing to do with what Dad eats." Rex explained to his little brother. "It's everything to do with how much he eats. Could you eat as much as Dad's been having for breakfast?"

"Not likely."

"Well there you are then. Quad bike a rat demon straddling[36]!"

Ran nodded.

He hadn't the foggiest notion either what was wrong with his Dad or what on earth his brother was rabbiting on about.

[36] He meant 'Quod Erat Demonstrandum'.

(Really)

When one is just six years old pretty much everything is a mystery. Some things were more mysterious than others. How in Heaven's Name was he ever going to get as brainy as Rex by the time he was eleven?

Although, come to think of it, that was a lifetime away. Well, one of his lifetimes, at least.

"Remember that Keep It Simple Stupid thing? Well, that's what we should do. This is the SIMPLE FACT: Dad is FAT because he eats too much." Rex told Ran.

"Got it."

"We've already helped an awful lot be making everyone[37] aware of it. But it's up to us to do more to help Dad. Agreed?"

"Agreed?"

And they did a fist bump. It hurt. Both of them. A lot.

In an ideal world, helping a loved one lose weight might mean quite a lot of suffering for that loved one, and maybe that jolly well serves them right, but NO SUFFERING for the helpers. Ran - or, more specifically, Rex - didn't see it that way. I'll explain why in a moment or two.

They did their research, those boys, and very good research it was too. Comprehensive and careful.

They made a long (and messy) list of all the BAD STUFF that was to be avoided. It became messy because Rex thought it would be useful to put everything in alphabetical order. Then they would be able to easily pick out 'things to steer clear of'.

They agreed that some of the food and drink to be given a wide

---

[37] By everyone, that means themselves, Mum, Dad, Nanny & Grandad.

berth were: cakes, biscuits, chips, burgers, pizzas, all other fast food, chocolate, sweets, bacon, snacks, sugary drinks, alcoholic drinks, fruit juice, fried food, white bread, diet soda, sugary cereal, white sugar, energy drinks, bottled water, sweets.

Okay, that might not sound a lot but just consider that 'sweets' encompass ALL of the boys' treats.

Not having pizza would RUIN their Saturday Film Night.

Not having chocolate would be nearly impossible!

It is a testament to Rex and Ran's love for their Dad that they were prepared to GIVE UP THE LOT if their Dad had to.

They may have been prepared to forego the whole list, but rather grudgingly and let's not pretend that they were happy about it.

They are boys, after all. Growing lads. The occasional treat was an innocent pleasure.

Just as an alcoholic, someone totally dependent on beer, whisky, wine and all the other strong drinks, CANNOT have even a single sip of anything stronger than tap water, so it would be with Dad.

No cutting DOWN for Dad.

Only cutting OUT for Dad.

No cutting DOWN for Rex and Ran.

Only cutting OUT for Ran and Rex.

Fair's fair.

And if that isn't love then, by golly and holy guacamole[38], I

---

38   Guacamole/Avocados are a great way to increase your intake of health-promoting nutrients like monounsaturated fats, fibre, folate, and potassium.

don't know what is.

"We don't really need sweets." Rex told his brother.

Ran was not convinced. He was not, as they say, sold on the idea. "Don't we?" He wondered.

"Nah!" Rex said: "We don't need cakes, biscuits, chips, burgers, pizzas, any fast food, chocolate, sweets, bacon, snacks, sugary drinks, alcoholic drinks, fruit juice, fried food, white bread, diet soda, sugary cereal, white sugar, energy drinks, bottled water OR sweets."

"Are you sure?"

"Yes."

"Say them again." Ran urged.

"Cakes, biscuits, chips, burgers, pizzas, any fast food, chocolate, sweets, bacon, snacks, sugary drinks, alcoholic drinks, fruit juice, fried food, white bread, diet soda, sugary cereal, white sugar, energy drinks, bottled water OR sweets."

"Abjuring all of those seems rather excessive." Ran told his brother in a very grown-up voice.

"Look! I've told you. If you was an alcoholic and had even one sip of beer or whisky or something YOU COULD DIE."

"Yes, but I'm not an alky lollik." Ran reminded him.

"That's not the point. If Dad STARTS eating that RUBBISH he'll get FATTER and FATTER. Why, just one tiny nibble of one little piece of chocolate could be a DISASTER."

Ran knew full well what a DISASTER was. Goodness knows. He was six and had had his fair share of disasters and definitely didn't want his Dad to have any.

Rex & Ran Save Their Dad

Cor! The disasters Ranulph had experienced already in his life. Too many to mention!

What about the time his BEST EVER DRAWING had been put up on the wall at school so that EVERYBODY could see it? And what had happened? A cleaning lady had ripped it with the end of her mop and thrown it in the bin!

What about the time Grandad had clawed his back with his sharp nails so badly that the marks were still there THE NEXT DAY?

What about the time he'd given Meg a biscuit and she'd BITTEN HIS FINGER? It really hurt but everyone just carried on talking about grown-up things as though nothing had happened.

What about the time he'd burnt his hand on Nanny's hot saucepan? Nanny had kissed it better, admittedly, and put some butter on it - which stank worse than dog poo.

What about the time he'd gone on an endless car journey and felt so sick that Dad had stopped the car for him to be sick? Unfortunately, he didn't quite make it out of the car before his breakfast came up. Dad told him that there were always bits of carrots in sick - and it was true, although he couldn't remember eating any carrots for weeks! An interesting point from Dad nevertheless.

Ran didn't really understand what an alcoholic was, although he expected that Smelly Grandad might be one.

Or Wise Grandad, because Dad said that alcoholics talk a load of rubbish and gibberish. That was mostly what Wise Grandad

(Really)

seemed to do.

"Let's give it a try ... and if we don't like it, we can give up giving up." Ran suggested.

"No! We can't! Dad will be relying on us." Rex told his brother. "If we give up that could be curtains for Dad. You don't want that, do you?"

Although Ran had no idea what curtains had to do with anything, Rex did make it all sound deadly serious, so he shook his head.

He really, really, really hoped that Dad would be unfatted very soon.

When he thought about it, no sweets didn't sound so bad ... at the moment.

Nor did it to Rex ... at the moment.

So they crumpled up their empty crisp packets, savoured those last few pieces of chocolate, stuck the final few Wotsits in their mouth, swallowed the penultimate wine gums, finished off the liquorice allsorts and swigged down their Fanta and Vimto.

Yep. No cakes, biscuits, chips, burgers, pizzas, all other fast food, chocolate, sweets, bacon, snacks, sugary drinks, alcoholic drinks, fruit juice, fried food, white bread, diet soda, sugary cereal, white sugar, energy drinks, bottled water and ... err ... sweets were not going to be a problem for these stalwart lads. Well, maybe the sweets, but NOT the rest.

Although ... come to think about it, what would Saturday Film Night be without pizza.

Gosh, even if they did just sneak a few sweets and pizzas in, there were still absolutely OODLES of things they'd be giving up to help their Dad. Devouring the odd pizza or a handful of sweets was neither here nor there in the Grand Scheme Of Things.

Was it?

Sufferin' succotash!

Galloping gremlins!

Gadzooks!

Dagnabbit!

Phooey!

Shitake mushrooms!

Get a grip, boys! Start taking this seriously. Time is running out for YOUR DAD!

(Really)

17

Those boys did get a grip!

Their chief helper - though not the only helper, by any means - was Smelly Grandad.

He had plenty of incentive. Apart from ... errr ... now then ... what's that slushy word? Oh, yes ... LURVE!

Well, that aside, there was also the FOOD.

Nanny and Grandad were ON A PENSION so they obviously lived hand to mouth, on the breadline, with barely enough money to get through each week.

Indeed, Nanny showed the boys her purse one Wednesday (the day before Pension Day) and all that lay within it were two ha'pennies[39] ... and a dead moth.

What a meagre haul!

"Never be able to tell anyone that you haven't got two ha'pennies to rub together.[40] Keep a couple in your purse or pocket and you won't go far wrong."

Usually it was Grandad who had these strange, old sayings that were totally meaningless but, sometimes, Nanny could surprise the boys with one.

Anyway, back to Grandad's food incentive.

All of the grub Dad usually had for breakfast - pork sausages,

---

39 Properly called a halfpenny. Worth, in today's money, sod all.

40 That means they're poor ... and it's written here in black and white so it must be true.

streaky bacon, baked beans, tomatoes, fried bread, fried egg, black pudding, white pudding, mushrooms, kidneys, hash brown, bubble & squeak, cheese tomato ketchup and brown sauce - were 'donated' to Grandad.

'Donated' by the simple expedient of STEALING it (or LIBERATING it, the boys preferred to say) and carrying it across to Nanny and Grandad's house.

And very much appreciated that lot was too!

Funny as it may sound, Dad NEVER mentioned a single word about his missing food.

Funny as it may sound, Ran and Rex never worried about poor, old Grandad getting FAT. Very odd.

Whilst Grandad was salivating over the luxury of all that food, all for himself, the boys took the opportunity to go for STAGE TWO of their plan to GET DAD SKINNY (and take away much of life's enjoyment but, in return, helping him to live longer and play more).

"Grandad?" Rex said.

Grandad tore himself almost physically, but mostly mentally, away from his dreams of luscious, never-ending meals. "Yes, lad?"

"We thought we might enrol Dad in a gym."

"Good idea. Jolly good idea."

It needs to be admitted that Grandad wasn't really listening because he was just too focussed - obsessed some might say - on all of that delicious food.

"Do you know of any?" Ran asked.

(Really)

More tearing away occurred. "Hmm! Let me see now. Well, yes, as a matter of fact I do."

"Can we go there, Grandad." Rex wanted to know.

"I don't see why not. Let me just get Nanny to store this ... this ... smorgasbord of delights. This gallimaufry of wonder. This potpourri of colluvies[41]."

The 'heart attack on a plate' was safely stored away before Grandad was prepared to do another single thing.

The gym was a huge disappointment right from the start.

When they reached the building, it looked derelict. The entrance door was practically hanging off its hinges and its wood was rotting and the paintwork may once have been a golden hue - but not any longer.

Where the colour could be seen, and that was not in many places, it reminded Ran of that incessant car journey where he'd deposited his breakfast. Imagine that without the carrots and you'll have a good idea of the unpleasant shade of vomit the door now was.

The large, old building had numerous small windows, each about the size of a standard sheet of paper. A lot were broken whilst the rest appeared to be held together only by spiders' webs and ingrained dirt. Some had rude words etched in them by small fingers and those windows, at least, allowed a minimal amount of light into the interior.

---

41   Grandad meant to mean 'a load of wonderful food' but this really means a jar of filthy fragrances.

Rex & Ran Save Their Dad

The gym's signage, once a vibrant, multi-hued, colourful, neon extravaganza, was a sheer disgrace. The supply of electricity to it was long gone. The march of time, and those same spiders' webs and muck that the windows bore, had transformed it from a thing of beauty into a contemptible and disgraceful shadow of its former self.

Worse, several letters appeared to be missing. Not just unlit, but completely gone.

The gym honoured the great American country singer, Willie Nelson, and his very first album, 'And Then I Wrote'.

The boys and their Grandad didn't know that, of course, although the evidence was there, right in front of them.

The gym name - Willie's Album - up there in lights for everyone to see, for ever.

Meaningless, but certainly a distinctive name.

Except the lights had been switched off for years, possibly decades.

Except the missing letters no longer spelled 'Willie's Album', thanks to the absent letters.

To all intents and purposes, the gym was now called 'Willie bum'.

At least it made the boys smile.

Indoors was no better. The place stank.

Imagine a hairy, old man who hasn't washed for a month, but who has sweated every second of every day, and never changing his clothes. The same underwear. The same socks. Ugh!

Rank, stinky and dark.

(Really)

That just about summed up the place.

And if Rex and Ran thought that the stench was just about bearable ... when Grandad shoved them just a few paces inside, WOW!!

What a miasma of mephitis and malodour!

No long car journey needed for Ran to be sick - just a few more minutes in this place would do the trick.

As for Rex, he of sterner stuff, his eyes began to bulge out of his head before he clapped his hand over his mouth.

For once, he was truly grateful that he'd excavated all of the ear wax out of his ears that morning and wiped the detritus off his finger nails into the palms of his hands.

He now had the delicate aroma of cerumen[42] in his nostrils instead of the appallingly putrid fetor of the gym.

That ... what should we call it? ... STINK had permeated everything, living and inanimate, over decades. If not decades, then over thousands of years. At least, that's what it seemed like.

Even Grandad's farts paled by comparison. It was like comparing the gentle waft of aromatic flowers with the bottom eruptions of a million cows with diarrhoea.

Did men really smell like this?

Ran and Rex each had but a single thought 'I don't want to grow up and be a man!'

Well, not a single thought, because they also had:

'Let's get out, quick!'

42   Scientific name for earwax - pronounced "seh-RUH-muhn".

and

'I'm going to puke!'

and

'I wonder if I can bottle this and sell it?'

That was Grandad who, I have to say, found it all rather nostalgic. It reminded him of his youth, when he'd lived in a hole in the ground with his Mum, Dad, twelve brothers, three sisters, and four other families[43]. Happy days.

"Yes, mate." A voice said.

To say that the owner of the voice was UNUSUALLY BIG would be an understatement.

From side to side, he was equally as wide as two Grandads. He had no discernible neck. His bare arms were so muscular that he appeared to have large pumpkins under the skin. His veins were so prominent that they might have been a map for the River Amazon's tributaries. His legs were very similar to tree trunks. His head was the same shape as a basketball.

The only thing that stopped him from being truly terrifying, from making the boys step back in sudden fear, was the fact that he was just, almost exactly, the same height as Rex. More or less, anyway, if not quite as tall. Nearly, though.

A man of amazing shape but, I'll bet, no-one ever poked fun at his short stature. Not more than once. Probably because, that first time, they'd end up in intensive care at the hospital.

"My Grandsons are interesting in treating their Dad to a membership." Grandad told him.

---

43   It's my book, so I can write whatever I like!!

(Really)

"Good idea, lads."

"We've got some money, but we don't really know how much it costs." Rex told him.

How strange it was, talking to a FULLY GROWN man eye-to-eye.

And, what a deep voice he had.

Ran was fairly certain that the man winked at Grandad.

"How much have you got, my little friend?"

"Three shillings and fourpence." Rex told him.

"And I've got tuppence!" Ran added.

Three and six[44]! What goodies the boys could buy with that? Where was the prohibited list again?

Ah, there it is ... cakes, biscuits, chips, burgers, pizzas, all other fast food, chocolate, sweets, bacon, snacks, sugary drinks, alcoholic drinks, fruit juice, fried food, white bread, diet soda, sugary cereal, white sugar, energy drinks, bottled water and ... err ... sweets.

Three and six would buy most of those. Not the alcohol! But, then, who on earth wants beer or wine or whisky?

"Three and six!" The gym man said. "By heck, that's a fair old lump of dosh!"

"Would it be enough?" Rex wanted to know.

"Might be. Might be. Tell you what, lads, you go and have a good look round and I'll have a chat with the responsible adult." He chuckled.

Rex and Ran looked round. There didn't appear to be anything

---

44   In 'new' money that's 17.5 pence.

they'd want to see. Except the way out. They certainly couldn't spot a responsible adult.

"Off you trot." The man said. "Oh, and you might like to leave the cash with me."

There really was no 'like' about it, but the man was an adult after all and he was holding out his hand, so Rex deposited his three shillings and fourpence in the grimy mitt.

And, if you think the sly old dog had forgotten Ran's tuppence, you're very much mistaken.

His other hand snaked out, the fingers waggled in a soundless 'gimme' gesture and that was Ran's tuppence gone.

The fingers on his other hand waggled at them. This time the gesture was clearly dismissive and the boys had no choice but to meander away.

Crappity Frackity! There was very little to see.

Big-bellied men with hairy armpits dripping sweat and full of grunts were of no interest. Indeed, they were slightly scary.

The equipment consisted of old, scratched and scraped metal bars and weights that looked older than Grandad.

The floor was ancient bare concrete that was covered with a sweaty layer of damp, ingrained dirt. No doubt the dirt was because there were no cleaning staff. Nor ever had been. The damp had descended in rivulets from men's soggy bodies.

The lights, the few there were, were very dim and the boys couldn't really see where they were going, nor what they were treading in. Whatever was underfoot was gloopy, greasy and gooey.

(Really)

In short, it was the stuff of nightmares.

It was more like a medieval torture chamber than somewhere ordinary men and women would go to get fit.

In fact, as the boys looked around, there didn't seem to be any 'ordinary' men and definitely not a woman to be seen.

Everyone seemed to have bodies that were ... well ... DISTORTED as well as malformed and misshapen.

They couldn't wait to GET OUT!!!!

Thankfully, the gym man and Grandad came back.

"Here y'are then, lads. All sorted." The muscly man said.

"And, there y'go. A penny change."

'Whoop-de-do!' Ran shouted - in his brain.

"All sorted." Grandad told the boys.

It was over.

And the only thing that stopped Rex and Ran from running pell-mell (and that's jolly fast!) to the exit was their innate good manners.

They did, though, walk very, very, very quickly indeed.

And they didn't move their hands away from their noses until they were way, way, way outside. Well away from the stinky, pongy poo-pah! In the FRESH AIR.

18

Gosh! Didn't everything go well?

Well, since you ask. Not absolutely everything.

Poor boys. Rex and Ran spent day after day with the pangs of hunger griping in their bellies. It really was awfully difficult not to eat ... what was on the banned list again? Just remind us. Oh, yes, cakes, biscuits, chips, burgers, pizzas, all other fast food, chocolate, sweets, bacon, snacks, sugary drinks, fruit juice, fried food, white bread, diet soda, sugary cereal, white sugar, energy drinks, bottled water and ... err ... sweets.

The careful reader may have spotted that the alcoholic drinks have been deleted from the list, out of the boys' kindness really. They'd agreed that Dad could have an infrequent alcoholic drink - beer or lager, for instance. On special occasions ONLY. What a kind thing for the boys to agree.

Mind you, their ulterior motive in taking it off the banned list was that they COULDN'T STAND beer or lager. They were really UCKY, made their bellies sore, their mouth stink and really hurt going down their throats.

Also, there seemed no point in banning something that they didn't like anyway. The prohibited stuff ought to be things they'd really, really miss.

I've no idea when and where they drank alcohol in order to find out that it was awful liquid but I'm willing to bet that it was only the once.

(Really)

Until their late teenage years, at least. Then WOOHOO! it's great ... more, please!

Dad started going to the gym every day.

Dad started eating smaller portions of food and only stuff that was good for him.

Remember, everybody, that dieting isn't a piece of cake[45].

Gosh, it was all going swimmingly.

There was the small matter of Dad's unfortunate aroma.

Oh, let's not beat about the bush, let's call a spade a spade. It wasn't an aroma, it was a foul, obnoxious, abhorrent reek that Dad brought home with him after every gym visit.

Thankfully, he trained in old clothes and didn't have to wear the same outfit for work.

When he arrived home after his first trip, his squidgy trainers stuck to the carpet.

After that, Mum rigged up a clothes line in the yard and hung some old blankets (to hide Dad's 'bits' from the neighbours!) over it on gym days.

Dad had to strip off completely outside - never mind complaining about how cold it was! Then run indoors with nothing on whatsoever and rush upstairs to wash himself in cold water.

His 'training clothes', then had to be soaked overnight - outdoors - in a solution of baking soda, vinegar, bleach and curry powder.

---

45 Not a large piece anyway.

Mum then spent the following day with all of the doors and windows open, praying that she wouldn't get any complaints from nosy neighbours and expecting the council to call round ANY DAY.

The overpowering odour was far, far too strong to dissipate in one day. It lingered. It hung about. It loitered.

Thankfully, their house didn't get enormous amounts of visitors, which was just as well, because Dad, Mum, Rex and Ran got rather used to the smell - but their few visitors plainly did not.

Mum had to keep inventing reasons why the stench was NOT THEIR FAULT. In other words, she was forced to FIB.

Mum blamed the sewers.

Then she said a rat had been delivered with the coal and died somewhere.

Then she told people it was next door's cooking.

Next she implied that the fishmonger had sold her some mackerel that a local cat had then stolen and hidden somewhere in the house.

Then it was Grandad's pipe tobacco mixed with his aftershave that was blamed. I think Mum forgot about Grandad's beard when she came up with that one! I think Mum forgot that Grandad didn't smoke a pipe when she came up with that one.

Then she blamed her own children for keeping food waste in their bedroom.

Then poor Meg was at fault for (allegedly) rolling about in badger poo before she rubbed herself all over the furniture.

(Really)

Yes, Mum is certainly an equal opportunities FIBBER. She doesn't mind who she blames.

Really, Mum, that is too bad!

She never did blame Fragrant Nanny, though. Not once.

And, Mum, you're not helping Dad one bit by washing his clothes so that they shrink! Dad is absolutely convinced that it's not necessarily him getting bigger, but more likely his clothes getting smaller. He's dieting and exercising so he cannot still be putting on weight!

Grandad assured him that things always got worse before they got better. Remember The Blitz?

Whilst we're looking at the downside of Dad's efforts to lose weight, let's not forget the way he threw himself wholeheartedly into his gym and keep fit regimes.

Isn't that good I hear you say.

Well, what about PLAYING WITH HIS KIDS?

Wasn't that, for Rex and Ran, the whole point?

Perhaps Dad might as well stay looking like a blob of lard or a whale or an elephant seal, or a Gloucester Old Spot pig or a hippopotamus or Winnie the Pooh or a blobfish[46] or a Sumo wrestler or Jabba The Hut or porky Porkbelly or Pot-bellied Percy or a sofa-surfing, lazy, fat, lazy bones.

Because he certainly wasn't spending more time playing with his beloved children.

He was becoming OBSESSED with exercise.

46 Probably the world's ugliest animal!

Rex & Ran Save Their Dad

If there was even a spare minute in his day, he'd find some sort of exercise to fill it.

"What's your favourite exercise, Dad?" Ran asked one day.

"Chewing!" Although he WAS trying to forget that.

And, whilst we're on the subject of exercise and UNFATTING, what about his trousers? They'd need replacing, as they got too big around the waist for him, so that's more expense - what Dad was saving on food would have to go towards new clothes that actually fit him.

Trousers that didn't fall down when he walked were essential if he didn't want to be arrested for showing his nether regions[47] in public.

Oh, surely there's no more bad news?

That was the end of the bad news, was it? It's uphill all the way now. Sun and sangria ahead.

Unfortunately, there are the PHANTOM CRAVINGS. Desperation to eat ALL of those foods you're not allowed anymore! Does Dad think about Sausage and Bacon every second?

No. During the many other seconds, he's too busy thinking about ALL of the OTHER delicious food he can't eat.

Rex and Ran can fully sympathise with that BECAUSE THEY'RE MISSING THEM TOO!! Not the alcohol, obvs! Pretty much everything else on the banned list. It all seems so much tastier and more pleasurable than the 'GOOD' stuff. It

---

47   His bum.

(Really)

all seems especially tasty just because YOU CAN'T HAVE IT. Alongside PHANTOM CRAVINGS, Dad's enjoying (not!) CRANKINESS[48]! and joining those feelings is his sudden urge to keep removing his shirt.

That's because he's getting UNFATTED.

Removing your shirt in public is not quite as bad as having your trousers fall down, but it isn't nice. Imagine if ladies of a nervous disposition ever saw that. Or small, impressionable children. Or, worse still, one's scullery maid or boot boy.

Also on the negative side is Mum's bed-linen. It just can't stand up to the additional strain of Dad's sweat and body odour. It either rots away or, when washing it is attempted, falls into a patchwork of holes.

More expense!

Dad's balanced diet (not, as he'd hoped, a bottle of beer in each hand[49]) was improving his health, his weight and his fitness levels.

It was doing all of those things for Ran and Rex as well (except they didn't need it) but, for them, there was an additional benefit. Or drawback, possibly. It was, according to Rex, ruining their mental health.

The entire business was just as difficult for the kids. Perhaps even more so.

No more sleepovers ... because of the smell, which seemed to accompany them wherever they went.

---

48 Being miserable and short tempered.

49 Think about it!!!

Practically no friends any more ... as above.

Not a single sweet between them for ages and ages.

Worse, their friends won't share because THEY HAVEN'T GOT ANY FRIENDS.

Boys are genetically predisposed to Ablutophobia[50] but Rex and Ran were spending more and more time in the shower or the bath just ... TRYING TO GET CLEAN AND SMELL-LESS.

Worserer, Sefton Park School formed a special committee to vote whether Ran and Rex could be BANNED.

When The Special Committee couldn't reach a decision (as committees often can't) a FULL MEETING was speedily organised.

This was a jam-packed meeting which quickly became very acrimonious, bad-tempered, cantankerous and curmudgeonly. Some of those present had no idea which particular boys were held to be the smelly ones - to be fair, there could easily have been more than two contenders, mostly boys but a few girls as well ... and ONE TEACHER.

If anyone wanted to experience WAR without people actually dying, they should have attended that gathering. Public executions in ye olde times had less baying and screaming from the watching mob.

Luckily, the only arms and legs that were broken were on a couple of chairs. Splotches of blood turned out to be tomato

50   Fear of washing.

ketchup from an attendee's hotdog that had been squashed against his chest by the surging crowd.

How such a small, relatively insignificant matter can get blown up out of all proportion is truly amazing.

Thank goodness for FREE SPEECH.

When the matter eventually, at long last, in due course, came to a vote, a show of hands decided NOTHING.

A SECRET VOTE by ballot was agreed after even more raised voices and anger.

Parties were divided.

Those wearing hippy clothes were generally in favour of chilling and letting anybody do anything they wanted to, including covering themselves with foul-smelling ooze if that was their 'bag'.

All those wearing red were pretty unanimous in insisting on unionisation being the correct procedure before anything was decided.

Those clad mainly in blue felt that hanging the children, well outside the school premises, would be an excellent, and permanent, solution.

The few odd (and I do mean odd) participants wearing yellow or gold didn't really have an opinion. Some of those, not all, wanted the man with the hot dog to be expelled from the room. Others weren't sure or were ambivalent or indecisive or couldn't make up their minds. They argued that a vote should use proportional representation[51]. Then they went silent when

---

51   It's politics. Can't explain it and it doesn't make much sense.

they realised that proportional representation had nothing to do with a ballot to decide YES or NO.

At last, some basic form of agreement about a vote was reached. Paper and pencils were allotted. Either a TICK or a CROSS would do.

It was a SECRET vote so the results became known only to the two people counting them. We cannot be totally 100% certain of the outcome because the voting WAS secret. Only Miss Herbert and Mr Crowley, as adjudicators, ever saw those ballot papers - which were burned immediately after the count. Messrs Herbert and Crowley knew the truth. Would they ever have banned Rex and Ran regardless of which way the vote went?

Maybe.

Maybe not.

The teacher who suggested they could stay if they wore Tyvek® suits[52] and gas masks shall remain nameless ... but we know who you are! I'm not saying Cypress or Acacia or Kapok or Beech but definitely possibly maybe almost certainly some kind of tree.

It wasn't Mr Simson, I can tell you that, because he was still hoping against hope that, one day, he'd beat Rex at Chess. FAT CHANCE! He certainly couldn't if Rex was banned. Could he? Keep Rex in school! And Ranulph.

Come to think of it ... maybe it WAS Mr Simson? After all, if Ran stayed in Sefton Park, HE might beat his head teacher at

52   Worn by the Emergency Services to protect against chemical hazards.

chess. How embarrassing would that be?

We may never know for sure but let's give Mr Simson the benefit of the doubt.

Anyway, the boys were staying at school. YAY!

And the PTA was finding extra funds for Mr Amri to disinfect certain things so that no-one went home from school smellier than usual. Not that much smellier than usual. Except for the nameless teacher who probably would stay pretty darn-goshed stinky.

Worsererer, Dad wasn't going on holiday with them because he was running a half marathon.

Mum told the boys that she wasn't keen on driving all the way to Skegness by herself.

They might not have a holiday at all.

What could EVER be worsererer than that?

A Day Trip to 'Skeggy' by coach was suggested, but that idea fell as flat as a pancake. That may have been the highlight of Grandad's childhood, but today's parents expected, nay demanded, something a darned sight more than that!

Ran and Rex were very, very sad. No summer sand. No candy floss ... on the banned list anyway, kids. No having their photograph taken for sixpence and getting, in the post, their photo - with head and feet all in the shot (take note, Grandad!). No bucket and spade. No donkey rides. No toffee apples ... on the banned list anyway, kids. No paddling. No crabbing. No sunburn. No chips ... on the banned list anyway, kids. No ice-cream ... on the banned list anyway, kids ... and at least Ran won't get sphenopalatine ganglioneuralgia[53]. Besides which ice-creams (and chips) just encourage seagulls to steal. No Bonny Baby competition (Ran came sixth once[54] and has never been allowed to forget it). No funfair. No roll-a-penny. No knobbly knees competition (Grandad once came last and he was delighted with that! Especially as he had, for many years, suffered from genuphobia[55]).

Saving Dad's life was turning into a bit of a disaster.

Nothing worth having comes easy[56].

---

53 Getting a headache from eating ice-cream too quickly.

54 Sixth out of seven.

55 Fear of knees.

56 Said by Theodore Roosevelt, arrogant US president. Murderer of bears (hence Teddy Bear) and, in just ONE safari, lion, hyena, elephant, rhinoceros, hippopotamus, warthog, zebra, giraffe, buffalo, eland, bushbuck, oryx, wildebeest, hartebeest, gazelle, monkey, ostrich, bustard, crane, stork, pelican, crocodile, python and more!

(Really)

19

Still, let's look on the bright side.

There's bound to be one, isn't there?

The day the postman came with yet another stack of official-looking envelopes certainly didn't seem to be part of any 'bright side'.

After all, letters that came in stamped and embossed envelopes with crests on were almost always bills.

And, Dad, it's no good setting them to one side, or hiding them in a drawer, they've got to be paid.

That fateful day, most of those bureaucratic missives WERE bills. Oh, dear, Dad, more debt.

Any chance at all of a holiday had suddenly gone from 'very little chance' to 'no chance at all'.

One of those communications was not a demand for money.

That one bore a multi-coloured escutcheon[57] on the front. It was of top-quality parchment and the address was typed in clean lines that contained no spelling or grammatical errors.

Dad was impressed.

He pushed aside the remnants of his bowl of cinnamon-spiced quinoa and oats that he'd been enjoying for breakfast and slit the envelope open with a pair of scissors.

The letter was almost as beautifully constructed as its envelope.

Dad drew a sharp intake of breath when he read its contents.

---

57   a posh design like the heraldic crest of some great lord.

Rex & Ran Save Their Dad

Rex and Ran were gazing at him all agog.

"Who's it from off of of, Daddy?" Ran wanted to know.

Dad held up one finger for silence and continued reading.

'Gosh!' Rex thought 'This is something jolly important.'

At last, Dad laid the letter down on the table.

"Well, I never." he said.

"What, Dad?" Rex asked.

"Well, I never did!"

"What, Dad?" Rex asked again.

"Well, well, well." Dad mused.

Two boys said, with but a single voice: "WHAT, DAD?"

"It seems that my trip to the emergency hospital has thrown up a couple of problems."

"Oh, Dad!" Ran whimpered.

Dad looked at his two dear boys with love in his eyes. "Oh, don't you worry about me, I'm as strong as an ox. I've just got to arrange to go in for some tests, that's all." Dad told the boys in a voice dripping with reassurance and, hopefully unnoticed, tinged with a certain level of fibbing.

Boys can sometimes spot a fibber when they see one. Goodness, they've certainly had enough experience, what with a certain elderly, smelly relative and his tall tales.

On this occasion they didn't spot that Dad was telling a falsehood and carried on with their delicious homemade vegan cashew yoghurt. Ran, being Ran, was devouring vegan haggis with raw vegan cantaloupe and watermelon nigiri-sushi as well. Meanwhile, Dad sat there in a daze with his bowels liquefied

(Really)

and the many, many hairs on his neck standing up. Deep within his heart a morsel of fear stirred. It was a morsel of fear that was even more tasteless than the boys' breakfast fare.

Rex and Ran were at school on the day that Dad was booked for his hospital appointment. For them, it was just another day at Sefton Park, sitting by themselves in their classrooms and, at break time, being asked to play right out on the far, far reaches of the playground well away from everyone else.

Thankfully, for everyone else, it was not a windy day and their miasmic effluvia[58] did not spread too far.

Dad cycled to hospital, as part of his fitness regime, taking with him nothing other than a clean pair of underpants.

This was something Fragrant Nanny insisted upon. For reasons best known to herself, it was a constant worry that she might have an accident and be found by ambulance workers, or nurses or doctors, not to be wearing clean knickers.

Once at the hospital, Dad was shown in to the doctor with what seemed to him to be undue, and unusual, haste.

He had looked forward to waiting for absolutely ages so that he could sit, squirm and worry an awful lot.

At this point, it's worth remembering that medical practitioners like doctors and surgeons use very long words that are meaningless to normal folks.

Goodness, don't ask about their writing - which is totally unintelligible. It takes many years of practice to make it so.

58 Pongy gutbag stinky stink.

Pharmacists and chemist have special lessons in how to interpret that writing and there is a certain pride that they are able to read it when nobody else can.

For the benefit of the 'average' reader, with no medical training or, like Dad, an inability to understand words of more than two syllables[59], the doctor's prognosis will have to be written here VERY CAREFULLY and read by an adult EQUALLY CAREFULLY.

So here, in words of many, many syllables, is what Dad had to go through.

Dad endured an esophagogastroduodenoscopy.

Having his triglycerides levels checked quite vigorously.

Hepaticocholangiocholecystenterostomies came next to check connections from his gallbladder and costochondritis.

Some borborygmi was noted.

A conclusion was drawn that the fasciculation was caused by the doctor's cold hands, as was any horripilation and the involuntary movement of the levator labii superioris alaeque nasi.

If this all sounds IMPOSSIBLE that's because it jolly well is! Well, impossible to say it all.

Now, boys, if you're not sure how to pronounce some of those length, high-faluting words, just ask a responsible adult to read them - Mum, Dad, Teacher, Aunt, Uncle, Nanny, Granda ... err ... I wouldn't bother asking Grandad.

---

59   This is a genuine illness.

   It's proper name is Hippopotomonstrosesquippedaliophobia

(Really)

Dad was shocked and worried when several other white-coated doctors joined in with his examinations.

Dad was even more worried when a severe-looking, white haired gentleman wearing a tweed three-piece suit, a monocle and a stethoscope arrived.

Dad was terribly, terribly worried (though tried very hard not to show it) when two more distinguished gentlemen arrived. The examination table got very crowded, with Dad hemmed in on all sides. The discussion around him was quiet and full of long words that he didn't understand at all.

Finally, the group, having apparently finished prodding and poking, retired to one corner of the room where they spent absolutely ages conversing in low voice, nodding and shaking their venerable heads.

If this all sounds DEADLY SERIOUS that's because it could well be.

Dad, once in danger of exiting life early because he was so FAT could now be in medical trouble again.

What was perfectly true - and perfectly understandable - was that, after the test, with only the first doctor still present, Dad sat in front of him with hyperhidrosis.

YUK!!

Don't worry everybody, that's just the medical term for sweaty hands and that's fairly normal when anyone is waiting for news that they expect will be dire, dreadful, deplorable and distressing.

"Well, well, well." The doctor mused.

"What?" Dad asked, sloppily squishing his damp hands together.

"Well," the doc looked Dad straight in the eye "you've had some sort of miracle escape from an extremely traumatic disease that is normally life threatening."

Dad waited.

"It seems as though your sudden weight loss has saved your life."

Dad's eyebrow, the left one, lifted.

"We're convinced," said the doctor, speaking on behalf of all the worthy luminaries who'd jabbed and stabbed, "that you had Achalasia, sometimes called esophageal aperistalsis."

Dad nodded wisely. Dad actually nodded cluelessly.

Ignorant and oblivious, just the way he liked it.

"Yes, your lower esophageal sphincter was this close," here the doctor held his thumb and forefinger very close together with only the tiniest of gaps between them, "this close to total blockage. That was caused by the sheer amount of food being forced down your throat."

"I'm on a diet." Dad whimpered.

"Yes, that's pretty obvious."

"Am I going to ... you know?"

"Thanks to dramatically lowering your food intake, you won't." Dad was assured.

"Will I have to have a ... you know?"

"Nope." The doctor sounded quite sad and annoyed that he wouldn't have the opportunity to get Dad 'under the knife'.

(Really)

"Miraculously, your dyssynergia esophagus appears to have healed itself. Not only have you had a very, very rare disease that I've never come across before but it has inexplicably self-healed, which none of my esteemed colleagues have ever known recorded. You, sir, are a modern miracle."

Dad felt quite proud to have been the possessor of such a rare disease.

"All that you have now is a touch of peritonitis and we'll just give you a prescription for that for some run-of-the-mill antibiotics."

Deep disappointment from the doctor. Great relief from Dad.

And, you know what this means?

Dad's LIFE HAD BEEN SAVED by two lovely boys who worried about their dear Daddy getting too fat to play with them.

No double chins for Dad.

No wobbly belly for Dad.

No huffing and puffing for Dad.

No hair for Dad. Whoops! Cross that out!

20

That's it, then, isn't it?

End of the story.

Dad's been saved by Rex & Ran, so the title of the book has come true. 'Whoopee!' for the boys!

Oh! Hang about a bit!

Hold up!

Just a mo!

Sit tight!

Hold your horses!

Wait a sec!

There's more to come.

Remember the things that got worse, worserer and worsererer? Well, they didn't suddenly get better and betterer and bettererer. Rex and Ran still had to grit their teeth, harness their determination and put up with the lack of ... what was it again? Oh, yes, cakes, biscuits, chips, burgers, pizzas, all other fast food, chocolate, sweets, bacon, snacks, sugary drinks, fruit juice, fried food, white bread, diet soda, sugary cereal, white sugar, energy drinks, bottled water and ... err ... sweets.

Let's not forget the distinct lack of friends.

Let's not forget the distinct lack of playtimes with Dad.

Could anything get worse than worserer? Was life going to turn into sweetness and light?

(Really)

Well ...

One boy lost his leading role in a play about an old magician with a long, white beard.

What?!

Yep. All those children who used to be friends with him decided that the stench was just too much. Instead, he was allowed to be the Usher. To stand outside in the freezing cold and point the way for parents.

One boy didn't have a 'proper' birthday.

Oh, sure, he got presents. But birthdays aren't all about presents, are they?

What about a BIRTHDAY PARTY? Ummm ... nobody came. Oh, except one little girl whose Mum brought her to the wrong house. She left immediately. Holding her nose.

What about playing with friends and getting loads of presents from them? I know, I know, it's not ALL about presents, but ... well, SOME would be nice.

Oh, don't get me wrong, there were FAMILY PRESENTS. And some of those were jolly nice, but it's not quite the same without a good supply of friends as well on a boy's SPECIAL DAY.

And, take a look at the page opposite (to save your writer repeating himself!). None of those things either.

Spinach, Feta and Red Pepper Lattices weren't really a special treat.

Nor were Fishless Finger Wrap Bites or Chipotle Focaccia with Garlic Onion Topping or Edamame Soybeans or Chickpea

Fritters with Yoghurt.

Oh, they were ok, I suppose. It was nice of Mum to make such an effort.

But it wasn't exactly THRILLING and most unlikely to give anyone a sugar rush or get them so overexcited so that they couldn't sleep.

I mean, that's what birthdays are all about ... eagerness, exhilaration and enthusiasm eventually followed by tears, tantrums and temper.

Unless a boy goes stomping up to bed in tears, it can't have been much of a birthday, can it?

And there are plenty of others involved in Dad's Diet - not central to it, maybe, but on the periphery, out on the edges, catching some of the fallout. Whether they want it or not. Whether they deserve it or not.

Mum, for instance.

Poor Mum now has to put up with all three of her 'men' being mingy, miserable, mardy and mournful because, make no mistake, one man's diet is everybody else's pain in the butt!

It's Mum who has to devise new, interesting food and drink all of a sudden.

Who do you think has to console, hug and kiss three chaps who are DOWN IN THE DUMPS so much?

Who do you think has to take care of those stinky, ripe, rotted, reeking clothes of Dad's. And, by association, of the two boys.

(Really)

Who has to STAND BY HER MEN[60] just as the song says because 'sometimes it's hard to be a woman'.

Still, as we read in a previous story, Mum has kept Dad's life insurance policy up to date, so it's not all doom and gloom. And she's always got her work as a spy and triple agent, working for East Germany and the British Government and for Ukraine. Plenty to keep her busy.

Fragrant Nanny was the one person who was least inconvenienced by all the fuss and furore. Nanny just carried on as usual. If she ever noticed the effluvia, she doubtless blamed in on Grandad.

Wise Grandad didn't know anything about it, really, because he was too busy discussing learned matters with his chums. Anyway, his sense of smell was very poor indeed, thanks to an accident with strong chemicals in his youth, so stinky stinks were of no consequence to him.

Smelly Grandad was a bit perturbed by it all. His perturbation was partly because he half hoped that Dad would fail on his diet, give up on it for a little while and then go back to it. That way Dad would buy some more deliciously meaty food that he'd eventually give to Grandad. Yummy!

Grandad saw quite a lot of the kids - that's what came of living just across the road from them - and the smell was a bit of a problem, even for Smelly Grandad. Thankfully, he'd discovered that extra goose grease on his chest, with a bit of

60 Famous song by Tammy Wynette from when Nanny and Grandad were young ... well, youngish.

turpentine added, masked the stench quite adequately. It had the added benefit of keeping his chest warm right through the cold Winter months.

Probably Dad's diet proved unfairest of all on Rex and Ran's teachers at Sefton Park School. The dieting saga and all its attendant rigmarole was, after all, nothing to do with them.

That didn't make life in the staff room any easier.

Sides were taken.

Things were said that were better left unsaid.

Rulers were brandished.

If it was not war that had invaded the staff room, it was, at the very least, a series of unpleasant skirmishes.

All because some teachers - and we know who you are - stood up for a couple of defenceless little boys. And all because some teachers - and YES, we KNOW WHO YOU ARE - didn't stand up for two defenceless little boys[61].

Yes, those two poor boys were the main topic of conversation throughout the school for quite some considerable time.

But did anyone mention the stinky teacher?

No, they did not.

Did anyone whisper 'B.O' secretly into that teacher's ear?

No, they did not.

Lastly, but by no means leastly, there was Meg the dog.

Meg, it has to be said, quite liked sniffing poo - and certain poo, like rabbit poo, she'd eat - so smelly kids were not a problem

---

61   DISCLAIMER: None of this happened in REAL life on THIS Earth.

   All of this Earth's Sefton Park teachers are brilliant.

(Really)

for her. Indeed, she got quite adept at rubbing herself all over the boys to transfer their stink to her.

Overall, it was most definitely Rex and Ran who came off worst of all. They were only children and yet the WEIGHT of Dad's Diet was mostly on their shoulders.

What brave boys.

What a sterling example to everyone.

21

Yes, what a lovely pair of lads.

A good example to anyone. I can almost hear some beleaguered and stressed-out parents saying to their kids: 'If only you were more like that wonderful Ranulph and Rex!'.

Yep.

Or, in reality, NOPE!!!!

Children - even the best of them - can only hold within themselves a given amount of forbearance, patience, stoicism and fortitude.

Even the very best of children - like Ran and Rex - have a breaking point.

An invisible line past which they cannot go.

An invisible thread between them and the 'dark side'.

In our two boys, that thread had been pulled tight for quite some considerable time. That thread didn't have much give in it. That thread was not the strongest thread in the world. All it needed was to start fraying and weakening and getting worn and tattered and delicate. In short, it had worn as thin as their patience ... and that, if you didn't know it, was pretty darned thin indeed. It was thinner than Dad could EVER become.

There was no fat on that thread and, at precisely the same time, BOTH threads, Rex's AND Ran's, simply perished like old elastic bands, shrivelled up and fell apart.

There is an old expression - 'his temper frayed' - that is a

(Really)

description of how bad, criminal things were begun like hitting people. With someone's temper fraying.

What was, for our boys, the final straw that broke the turtle's back when it fell off the fence post?

What dire event put the cat among the eagles?

Well, it was a circumstance that, at first, sounded pretty, jolly good.

"I'm giving up the gym." Dad said one morning over breakfast.

Ran nearly choked on his tofu scramble (the one without the garlic powder).

Rex's mouth went so dry that his peanut butter[62] flapjack stuck to the roof of his mouth, rendering him incapable of speaking. Dad pretended to ignore the two pairs of eyes staring at him. If you ever want to see what eyes look like when they're ASTOUNDED just tell children something that is wildly unlikely but, they hope, believable. That's what astounded eyes look like.

No more stinky stinks!

No more ostracism[63]!

More playing with Dad!

More playing with friends!

The list of positive things was endless. Well, not exactly endless, but definitely EXCELLENT.

"Yes," Dad went on, "I'm not really getting it any more."

---

62 Arachibutyrophobia is the intense, irrational fear
    of peanut butter sticking to the roof of one's mouth

63 Being banned from a society or a group

Quite what Dad wasn't 'getting' any more was a mystery, but the kids didn't care. It would even be true to say that THEY DIDN'T GIVE A DAMN! And that's swearing.

"Yes," Dad went on dreamily, "it's all a bit basic ... and a bit ... basic. Yes, too basic. That's it."

"What does 'basic' mean, Dad?" Ran wanted to know. "Is it the same as stinky?"

"Not exactly. It means rudimentary[64]."

"Oh." said Ran.

Rex, still trying to extricate peanut butter from the roof of his mouth, said "ill goo pray widows gore[65]?"

"Ay?" said Dad. Which is not very polite.

But then it's not very polite to speak with one's mouth full of food. Not that Rex was bothered about his rudeness. At that precise moment, he was more concerned about his Arachibutyrophobia and the possibility of Dad having more free time to play with two non-smelly boys.

"Ay?" said Rex back. It is a source of wonder that the word 'ay' sounds much the same whether a mouth is full or empty.

"Yes, I'm joining another gym. It has MACHINES rather than just free weights. It has STEPPERS and RUNNING MACHINES. Plus, it has showers."

"Wow! Dad! Does that mean no pong any more?" Ran asked.

"It certainly does." Dad assured him. "Not only no pongy pong but I'll shower at my gym so instead of stenchy stench

---

64   Explain what this means, please, or the bit overleaf will be meaningless!

65   'Will you play with us more?'

it'll be scenty scent."

"Wow! That's great, Dad!" Ran shouted.

"Ehh! Mmmm!" Agreed Rex. That peanut butter was certainly gluey!

"'Course, it is a bit more expensive. But it'll be well worth it with all that extra equipment and ... NO NIFFS and HUMS! Won't that be great, kids?"

"Thanks, Dad." Rex said. The offending paste having, at last, been removed and swallowed. Although Rex didn't know it, the gluey stuff was very, very similar to the fixative Great Grandma had used to keep her false teeth in place.

For some reason Dad had that guilty look on his face.

You know, the one Mum knew about - whenever Dad had done something wrong!

Like spending money they didn't have.

Or ruining his clothes for no reason.

Or using all the toilet paper and not telling anyone.

Or not mowing the lawn when he'd insisted that he HAD.

Or not cleaning his bicycle.

Or not mending punctures so the kids discovered they STILL had FLAT TYRES.

It was unquestionably his guilty look.

Rex and Ran both recognised it. They had seen it before.

Dad was the embodiment of innocence when he said: "Obvs it's much more expensive so we might have to go without a few things."

Dear reader, let me translate that for you into PLAIN

Rex & Ran Save Their Dad

ENGLISH.

'We can't afford it. YOU (my children) will have to do without something.'

"That's alright, Dad. As long as you can play with us." Ran assured his Dad.

What a lovely, innocent child. Dad thought.

Rex, on the other hand, said nowt - but he narrowed his eyes and pursed his lips.

"Thanks, Rannie. Just as well we've decided not to have a holiday this year as we can't afford that as well my gym fees."

Hang about a bit!

Hold up!

Just a mo!

Sit tight!

Hold your horses!

Wait a sec!

'We' had decided not to have a holiday this year.

WE?

WE?

Rex didn't remember any 'we' in the decision.

Rex didn't remember any 'no holiday'.

One of the many wonderful things about being a child is that THE BRAIN hasn't filled up. Unlike Grandad's, for instance. That means that children remember more things and Rex was 100 percent sure that all Mum had said they 'might not' have a holiday.

That's not a 'no'. It's a 'maybe'. Or possibly a 'we'll see'.

(Really)

Anyway, what's wrong with getting a train or a coach to Skegness?

Rex was horrified to hear that Dad had suddenly turned that possibility of a holiday into a resounding NOT A CHANCE. Who passed wind and put Dad in charge?

"Right!" said Rex later.

"What does 'rude he meant to be' mean?" said Ran later.

"Right!" Rex repeated. "You need to concentrate, Ran. Because we need a plan."

"Will it be a 'rude he meant to be' one?"

"It might be."

Ran was none the wiser. All he knew was that his stomach was rumbling, Dad wasn't playing with him enough, he was fed up to the back teeth with being smelly, he had no friends, and was NOT going on holiday.

It's no wonder that the young of today have so much mental illness if all those are the sorts of things they have to put up with.

"I know!" Rex shouted. "We'll go on strike!"

"Like matches?"

"Not verzaktely."

"Like cobras?"

"No."

"Like meteors?"

"Shuttup, Ran. I'm thinking."

"Well, it can't be a hunger strike because we're already on one!"

"I'm still thinking, Ran, so please be quiet."

And Rex did think, using mainly his rather clever brain but also utilizing twiddling thumbs. He found that helped his concentration.

At long, long last, when his little brother was sinking into the slough of despond[66] and losing the will to live and in agony from his aching bum because he'd been sitting very still with hardly any wriggling about, Rex clicked his fingers. Well, he tried to. Didn't quite succeed.

"GOT IT!"

"Well, don't give it to me." warned Ran.

His older brother ignored that bon mot. It was, he thought, just the sort of silly thing a six-year-old WOULD say. He wished he'd thought of it.

"We'll go on strike and that means we'll withdraw our labour and not help with anything and not join in at all."

"Won't that be pretty horrible." Ran asked.

"Not really. We'll have stopped being so pungently aromatic - that means we won't be stinky - so we'll have lots of friends to play with again."

"And Dad?"

"No. That's the point. Dad's not playing with us because he'd rather go to a silly gym, lift stupid weights and do daft running."

"Yes, but we saved his life, didn't we?"

"Ran, that's not the point. It's not about saving someone's life.

---

66   Bored and depressed.

(Really)

It's about more important things than that. It's about NOT GOING ON HOLIDAY."

Rex's face was getting redder and redderer.

It reminded Ran of Dad's face when he had 'his little episode' at the bike park. Ran did not like it at all.

22

So strike those two boys did.

They made themselves as annoying as possible.

Wise Grandad didn't know anything about it, really, because he was too busy discussing learned matters with his chums. Anyway, his knowledge of children was very poor indeed, thanks to an incident with bullying siblings in his youth. So annoying annoyances were of no consequence to him and, as a general rule, he found it best to ignore children completely. If at all possible.

Smelly Grandad was not a bit perturbed by it all.

Fragrant Nanny remained blissfully unaware. The boys' demolishment of her Welsh cakes remained unabated.

So what, verzaktely, did the 'strike' mean?

Ran and Rex didn't make their beds each morning.

They didn't tidy up their rooms or put their toys away neatly.

They didn't go to bed the very first time they were asked.

They didn't wash behind their ears every day.

They didn't comb their hair in the mornings.

They didn't get home from school on time.

They didn't tell Mum and Dad what they'd done at school.

They didn't change their underwear every day.

They didn't help Mum with the shopping.

They didn't help Mum with the cooking.

They didn't help Mum clean the house.

(Really)

They didn't do any gardening.

They didn't eat all of the broccoli on their plates.

They didn't paint or draw their parents to resemble human beings.

They didn't take the rubbish out.

They didn't vacuum the carpets.

They didn't take off their muddy shoes outside the house.

They didn't help to hang out the washing.

They didn't clean their teeth properly.

They didn't do as they were told.

They didn't go in for tea when they were out playing.

They didn't listen to what Mum and Dad were telling them.

They didn't laugh at Dad's jokes.

They didn't send any 'thank you' letters for presents.

They didn't join a yoga class.

They didn't let Grandad win at chess.

And what does all that mean?

It means that NO-ONE NOTICED that Rex and Ran had gone on strike, that they'd withdrawn their labour in the best traditions of the downtrodden working classes.

Everything seemed - to everyone else - to be perfectly and utterly NORMAL.

As far as the adults were concerned, the two boys were no more annoying than usual. They were no more helpful than they'd ever been.

The moral of the tale is: there's no point in withdrawing your labour if there is NONE to withdraw.

Rex & Ran Save Their Dad

It wasn't THAT LONG before they decided not to bother with THE STRIKE.

What was wrong with adults?

Didn't they pay attention?

Didn't they care about the possible mental instability of their beloved children?

Or was it just because Rex and Ran didn't fully appreciate that they NEVER did any of those things they didn't do?

I'm betting on that last one!

Children don't realise how little they do - until they've got children of their own. By that time, IT'S TOO LATE!!!

Children also don't realise how much their parents do for THEM - until they've got children of their own. By that time, IT'S TOO LATE!!!

Rex and Ran sat at the kitchen table in Nanny and Grandad's house, with their heads in their hands, feeling gloomy and miserable, as Grandad explained all this to them.

"That's not true, Grandad!" Rex objected.

"We do LOADS, Grandad!" Ran confirmed.

"Let me go back to the previous page," said Grandad "and read out that great long list of 'They didn'ts' and you can tell me which you did do."

And he did.

And they couldn't.

That is, they couldn't admit that they did A SINGLE ONE of the things they didn't do.

Which quite surprised the boys. They'd never really understood all of the things they didn't do because they were too busy doing all the things they did do.

Grandad gave them a sheet of paper each and freshly-sharpened pencils.

"There y'go then, boys. Make a list of all the things you do do." He instructed.

And that's what they jolly well did do. They did do a 'do do' list.

"Crikey blimey!" Rex moaned, "It's not fair that EVERYONE thinks we don't do things THEY do do when we do do things they don't do."

And, after asking Grandad for extra sheets of paper (just in case) the two of them settled down very quietly to write their amazing lists.

Grandad sat equally quietly. So noiseless and still was he that he might just as well have been fast asleep. Oh, he was asleep!

When he eventually awoke, several hours had passed.

The boys had finished their Herculean task and gone home.

All that was left were a few cake crumbs, a dribble of squash in the bottom of their glasses and THE COMPLETED LIST.

The list started with ...

Hang about a bit!

Hold up!

Just a mo!

Sit tight!

Hold your horses!

Wait a sec!

Rex & Ran Save Their Dad

The paper's blank.

Completely and utterly blank!

Well, apart from a few squiggles which Ran did when he got bored. And his name, neatly written in the top, right-hand corner (with the capital 'R' the wrong way round like this Я).

Do you mean to tell me that they've given up and there are actually so few things on the 'do do' list? When I say 'so few' there were actually NONE.

Just checking ... yep, the other side's blank as well.

Well, young Rex, that's one idea you CAN take off the list. Strike off the strike idea.

(Really)

23

More successful was Rex and Ran's re-entry into 'normal' life. The smell that had wafted alongside them became a thing of the past. Their friends were back. They were soon being treated as though nothing had ever happened.

Rex wasn't given back the LEAD ROLE in his play because it had been promised to some other child and promises, as all good children know, may not be broken.

WELL, PERHAPS THEY SHOULD BE!!!!

He did have the consolation of being second understudy. That meant that, if two people dropped out for any reason, he'd get the part. Huh! Fat chance of that happening.

Oh, dear, one little boy contracted incipient diarrhoea the day before the play, so he was OUT.

Perhaps he shouldn't have been so greedy and eaten all of that huge bag of liquorice one of his kind classmates had left for him anonymously.

Oh, dear, one little boy lost all of his lines and couldn't practise without them. He could have sworn they'd been in his bag but, search as he might, there was not a sign of them. Half an hour before the play started he knew precisely NONE of his lines.

Rex, who had two copies for some strange reason, was able to step in and PLAY THE LEAD!

Ran drew an even better picture than his last one and it was put up in the school and adorned with TWO gold stars.

Rex & Ran Save Their Dad

Both boys had Recognitions in Assembly and both boys received 'Fabulous Friday' certificates.

If Mr Simson sniffed rather pointedly when he went past Rex and Ran, maybe it was because he'd lost at chess again and NOT because he was just checking that they didn't stink.

It was almost certainly NOT because he was a poor loser - just a considerate head teacher.

Their lives began to get back to normal. Or as normal as it was possible to be under the circumstances.

Money was tighter than before. That was a definite blot on the horizon.

Mum and Dad told the boys that they'd have to tighten their purse strings and tighten their belts. Rex and Ran didn't think that was very fair as their Dad was loosening his belts, so why should they tighten theirs?

Not that Rex and Ran really and truly understood all that stuff about money, as their concept of monetary and financial matters was limited. Amortisation, bounded rationality, diminishing returns, inflation targeting, macroprudential regulation, oligopoly and Seigniorage were as meaningless to them as they are to both the writer of this and the reader.

Let me, then, try to explain Mum and Dad's monetary economics in simple terms, if I can.

Payments out UP! and Payments in - DOWN! = DISASTER.

What on earth were all those new Payments out?

Well, Dad's selection of new trousers, in which the waistband actually fitted his waist. Perhaps he should have kept the ones

(Really)

where the belt was tighter?

Dad's extortionate gym membership fees.

The gym kit Dad 'had' to wear in the posh new gym.

The 'special' training shoes Dad 'had' to buy for his running.

Let's not mention the half-marathon (more on that later) vest, tracksuit bottoms, special padded underpants, nipple covers[67] and anti-odour, anti-sweat socks.

But Dad was happy, so Mum was contented as well.

Gradually ... so gradually that a snail moved faster (so the kids thought) life was returning to normal.

Dad actually shouted at his children one morning. It was not as though they'd done anything wrong. Not really. Toilets sometimes overflowed, didn't they? Did that mean it was Rex and Ran's fault for conducting a SCIENTIFIC EXPERIMENT to see how many complete rolls of loo paper would fit down the toilet bowl?

Did that justify such a tongue-lashing?

Those dear children just thought to themselves how quickly Dad had forgotten that they had SAVED HIS LIFE!! Every day he lived, it was thanks to his two sons. Ha! All forgotten! Life was not fair!

But the snail, or tortoise if you prefer, did keep moving forward and Dad did start playing with them a bit more.

Not if he was gymming.

Not if he was running.

---

67   Essential unless you have sufficient hair on your chest to protect nipples from being rubbed by your running vest. Sore nipples! Arrggh!

Rex & Ran Save Their Dad

Nor if he was working.

Nor if he was exercising.

Nor if he was performing Tai Chi in the rec.

Even if Rex and Ran were in the rec with him, he'd be struggling with his 'White Crane Spreads its Wings' or 'Repulse Monkey' rather than 'Man Lets Boy Score Goal' or 'Boy Kicks Man Painfully In Shin'.

But, nevertheless, playing a little bit more each week.

And how fit their father was becoming.

He might even be fit enough to win the Fathers' race at the school sports day.

Moreover, whilst his biceps weren't so muscular that he appeared to have large pumpkins under the skin, there were certainly a couple of tiny Brussels sprouts ... or garden peas?!

The wheezing and shortness of breath was a thing of the past (like Dad's THANKS to a couple of boys for SAVING HIS LIFE, apparently! That seemed to have been forgotten in the mists of time even before time had actually misted over!).

Grandad had regained his somewhat dubious title of Number One Farter. A source of pride for him - though not for another single person on the planet.

So most of our 'heroes' are happy. Not Fragrant Nanny, obvs, re. her husband's regained title.

As everyone stumbled back to normality it soon seemed that Dad's episode, his FATNESS and THE STINKINESS was like a myth or legend and the boys sometimes wondered if it really had all happened.

(Really)

They were a resilient pair of lads ... although they had their struggles over the next few weeks.

Ran stopped going to the toilet at home and would save it for school or for the garden. He'd been dreaming that there were giant snakes down the loo and he was frightened they'd bite him.

Quite where he got that idea from was completely unknown.

Rex, the success of his acting having gone to his head, spent far too many hours practising, over and over, the speeches he'd given (both his Mum and Dad were given free headaches, thanks to that). Unfortunately, trying to negotiate the stairs with eyes raised to heaven and arms flailing about, was not a success. He fell down the stairs and although his pride was hurt most, his body was not badly damaged.

He did get an ecchymosis (it's rather similar to a periorbital haematoma) of which he was extremely proud. Until he discovered it was just a posh word for a bruise.

Then, as if the boys felt that things could not get any better, the unthinkable happened.

Dad decided that running was too much like hard work. Especially if it was cold, or dark, or raining. Or if a coal fire was blazing in the hearth. Or if tea had been extra-specially good (didn't happen very often, particularly if it was goats' cheese tart with broccoli sauce). Or if, as was happening more and more, he just didn't fancy getting up of his lazy butt. So his marathon training tapered off and he suddenly decided that thirteen miles of torture and pain was, perhaps, not such a good idea after all.

Did anybody care? Were Rex and Ran bothered in the slightest?

YES, THEY WERE!!

Because they were going on holiday instead.

After all that talk of not going.

Maybe the kids' strike had worked after all.

It was more likely that Dad was feeling a bit guilty about not playing with them as much as he might. Maybe he really did want to thank them for SAVING HIS LIFE.

Not that Ran and Rex ever went on and on and on about it. Nobody wants to be constantly reminded that some children SAVED HIS LIFE.

There's no doubt that the boys did think that Dad had forgotten that they'd SAVED HIS LIFE.

And they didn't want to keep harping on about it, just because they'd SAVED HIS LIFE.

Err ... no ... he had quite mislaid that fact from his mind. They were going on holiday because Mum and Dad fancied visiting the seaside for a change and because Nanny had persuaded Grandad to donate TEN SHILLINGS to the holiday fund in payment for all the food the kids had given him. Err ... sorry ... stolen for him.

With that sort of cash available - although things were still pretty tight (see: purse strings and belt ... and Grandad's being tight fisted in not giving a pound), it meant they could have a fantastic, super deluxe holiday.

Yes, a day trip to Skegness!! Whoopee!

(Really)

Mum's not driving!! Whoopee!

It's a coach journey!! Whoo ... err ... that means Ran will be sick. Oh, dear!

No. Mum's had a word with the driver and Ran's going to sit RIGHT AT THE FRONT. Whoopee!

They had to get out of bed at 3 o'clock in the morning. Not a whoopee there then.

The coach took FIVE HOURS to reach Skegness.

Another vote for no blasted whoopee!

Crikey-blimey would they ever, ever get to the seaside?

"I CAN SEE THE SEA!" Ran shouted. That was the great thing about sitting right at the front. He could see everything before anyone else.

They were at the seaside!

The sea was right there. Just in front of them. The sandy beach was just a few steps away.

Their journey had taken forever and now they had to wait another forever for the coach driver to finish chatting to everybody and open the luggage hold. Then the boys were LAST to be given their buckets and spade.

FINALLY, they dashed across the road with Mum and jumped onto the sand.

It was wonderful. It was marvellous. It was amazing. And the heavy rain didn't bother them a bit. Well, hardly at all.

Mum cowered under her umbrella and snuggled down into her pac-a-mac as much as she could.

Dad had to pop across the road to the pub, just to make sure that the beer was drinkable. Apparently, he'd promised to report that back to Grandad. Not that the boys understood that at all because Grandad didn't drink beer, or come to that, any alcohol at all.

Still, when you're busy playing on a REAL BEACH you're not too concerned about the possibility of Dad becoming an alcoholic.

It was A REAL BEACH that the boys had all to themselves. Not another family anywhere to be seen.

What an amazing feeling.

How incredible is that?

That's Skegness for you!

Surprising really that black skies and a bit of thunder and lightning would put people off. If anything it made the boys' sand castles stick together better - what with all the rain. And the lightning added quite a bit of atmosphere to the task of breaking their forts and castles apart. Who needs real cannon when you've got a good helping of genuine thunder.

What a day!

And, if the candy floss was more sickly than they'd remembered, it didn't matter.

If the apples inside the toffee were bruised and maggoty, so what?

If the bag of chips went mostly to marauding gulls, it was of no account. The chips were so greasy that little fingers couldn't hold them anyway.

If the public toilets were disgusting and stank horribly, what of

146

(Really)

it. They had an entire beach to poo on.

If the crane in the arcade didn't EVER EVER pick up a toy, did it spoil the fun?

If the coach driver was an hour late coming back to the coach, never mind. Ran watched him weaving his way down towards the coach from the pub where he'd spent the day.

And, finally, if Rex and Ran had to give the driver a tip when they got home, did it ruin their day?

Yes, it blasted well did because he was a drunk driver who might well have KILLED THEM and he definitely did not deserve the tuppence EACH they gave him.

He seemed to realise that, too, judging by the glum expression on his face when they handed it over.

If he had KILLED THEM then what would have been the point of SAVING DAD'S LIFE. Not that they were going to mention that yet again once more.

No. Their holiday day was superb.

What lucky lads they were to have a whole day at the seaside. I say a whole day, but if the five hour journey getting there was taken away, and the seven hours getting home (the driver got lost in the dark, because he was befuddled) then they had more than TWO HOURS in Skegness.

That's more than enough for most people.

It was certainly more than enough for Ran and Rex who spent the greater part of the return journey fast asleep.

Didn't they have a great day? Well, the very next day Grandad could tell that they definitely had by the fact that their faces and necks were bright red.

That's something unique to Skegness. Visitors can go home with a case of sunburn even when the sun hasn't been out.

Mum had thoroughly enjoyed herself because she hadn't done a single bit of housework or cooking for the entire day. Not only that, but she'd managed to pass on a bit of useful information to one of her spy contacts from Ukraine.

"У четвер, 24 числа, Володимир Путін буде у Волковому районі Луганська[68]." (phonetically: "U chetver, 24 chysla, Volodymyr Putin bude u Volkovomu rayoni Luhans'ka.)

And, to muddy the waters in East Germany, she'd sent, anonymously, the same message in German - "Wladimir Putin wird am Donnerstag, den 24., nicht im Bezirk Wolkowa in Luhansk sein."

Oh, not quite the same message because the word 'not' had been added. That'll confuse those communists!

Isn't it nice that Mum has a second job?

Dad had had a high old time as well, helped enormously by several pints of Kilt Lifter, a rather hoppy craft beer from America. Plus the fact that he, alone of the family, was not dripping wet from being out in the thunderstorms.

The coach had stunk of damp gaberdine all the way back from 'Skeggy' but the boys were oblivious. They remained in the arms of Morpheus for the entire trip.

Everything was just about back to normal. Back to the pleasures

---

68   Vladimir Putin is going to be in Volkova District,

Luhansk on Thursday the 24th.

of being in the family before Dad got FATTED.

Ran and Rex had really missed those simple, yet enjoyable, pleasures. And the lovely, hilarious games they always used to play with their Dad were coming back.

Playing King Of The Bed again without bouncing off Dad's huge, fat belly and landing on the floor in great pain.

Playing 'Name That Tool' with Dad and his toolbox ... and a very thick pair of gloves on AT ALL TIMES. You know what happened last time? Yes, Dad cracked his head open when he fainted at the sight of all that blood.

The Barbecue Relay Race - but why not play it when you're getting all the barbecue stuff out, not when it's red hot and you're putting it away.

What's In Dad's Wallet? - a variation on the original 'How Many Moths In Grandad's Wallet?'. Each correct item written down gets a point!

Blindfolded Obstacle Race ... err ... after what happened last time? You've got to be joking. That game is consigned to history!

Pie Eating Contest. Err ... nope! It might still be Dad's favourite but not when he's on a diet. Anyway, he always, always won.

Tackle Daddy. Rather like 'Kick Dad In The Shins' but any part of his body can be tackled except his delicate bits. May be combined with the Wrestling Game but bear in mind the simple rule that only Dad can be hurt ... and the smallest player, obvs.

Hide and Seek. Not a great favourite since the last time Rex and Ran played it with Nanny. She ripped up two floorboards and hid underneath for two days. The boys ended up in floods of tears because, just like the time they lost their favourite football, they thought it was their fault. Poor boys. Poor Nanny for having to stay under the floor for all that time. If Grandad hadn't heard her sneeze she might still be waiting under the floor.

Poor Grandad too. He had to make his own tea for TWO DAYS. To be fair he wasn't worried about Nanny, he just thought she had gone out shopping, had run into a friend and stayed chatting without realising how the time was flying past. For TWO DAYS, Grandad? You're having a laugh!

The two boys sat, one Saturday evening, cuddling up to Mum and Dad, watching The Lone Ranger on their black & white television, enjoying vegetarian pizza.

Both boys had picked off the artichokes, the bell peppers, the baby spinach, red onions and cherry tomatoes but the cheesy pizza dough was still really nice. Well, quite nice. Well, edible. Well, edible if you were really hungry.

Rex said: "Isn't it great that we're all one big, happy family?"

"Deffo!" said Ran.

Dad nodded.

"I love our family!" Ran said.

"Me too as well." agreed Rex. "It's the best family in the whole wide world!"

Dad nodded.

"What do you think, Mum?" Rex asked.

(Really)

"Mmm ..." said Mum "let me just think about that for a few minutes."

Printed in Great Britain
by Amazon

33284762R00086